BRUMMELL'S LAST RIFF

Alan Fletcher

First Published by Chainline 1995

149, Hilton Road, Mapperley, Nottingham, NG3 6AR

ISBN 0 9526105 0 7

British Library Cataloguing in Publication Data.
A catalogue record for this book is available from the British Library.

Typeset by:- Margaret Hitchen
and
Sharespace Management Ltd, Nottingham:

Jo Burt
Dawn Berresford
Lynne Holland

Printed by Carson Offset Ltd, Lilac Grove, Beeston, Nottingham.

1. BRUMMELL'S LAST RIFF

2. THE LEARNING CURVE (ISBN 0 9526105 7 4)

Also by Alan Fletcher - **Quadrophenia** - The Novel (Corgi 1979)

Cover design: Andrew Findern

MODernisms

The three main characters in the book are **loosely** based on living persons - they should recognise themselves from certain traits of personality - if they can't then I've failed in this respect.

Some of the events in the story actually happened, some are reflections and embroideries of actual events (and may not necessarily have happened to the characters in the story), and some are pure figments of imagination.

It should be noted that this is a story of a time which was pre-political correctness, pre-feminism and (for many of us) pre-cious. The decision was taken to reflect the authenticity of the period in which the book was **set (**and its ambience and attitudes) rather than dilute it by tempering with the protocols of the decade in which it was **published.**

The book is dedicated to the spirit of the mid-60s, created by all the Mods (and the Rockers) and those named in the following paragraphs. There will be many others, not mentioned here, whose names I have either forgotten or never even knew, but whose faces are indelibly etched in the memory of those days. The book belongs equally to them as to the people named below:-

Newark:-

Dave Hill, Paul Mitchell, Frank Snyder, Tony Greenberry, Steve Greenberry, Janice Richards, Lynne, Chris Lawson, Howard Thomas, Pete Smith, Maureen Coomber, Cathy Ginelly, Sue and Diane Wright, Janet Cranidge, George Bower, Paul Cook, Ian Baker, Ellie Smith, Dick (from Brant Broughton), Kerri Howell, Adele Whitely, Bridget Onn, and all the Convent girls, Robert Weekley, George Kimberley, Malcom (Twig) Wing, Dave Kimberley, Paul Kimberley , Paul (Sam) Salmon, Trudi Healey, Didi, Alan Tinsley, Jill Holden, Barry Howell, Margaret Kimberley, Jackie Payne, Jimmy (the Beatnik) Walters, Bruce Richardson, Jimmy (Clean) Parker, Jenny Ancliffe, Diana Jones, John (Butch) Faulds, Jock, Phillip Goy, Roy (Lemon) Slater, Mick Walker, Meg Bentley, Pat Baines, Barry Hubbard, Danny Bentley, Teddy Johnson, Panic Payne, Tony Severs, David Townrow, Rita Cannon, Brenda Picker, Mick Joynes, David (Tomo) Thomson, Bobo and his Ducati (the only remembered Rocker), Jeff Lovatt, Eugene Lovatt.

Grantham:-

Judy Lambley, Vivien Smith, Carol Gribbon, Magdalene Buxton, Hannah Buxton, Frances Gilbert, Paula Cudmore, Georgina, Jill Garrard, Pat Hill, Mary Jones, Pam Hill, Jennifer Nussey, Angela Mahoney,Julie Hallam, Pete Geeson, Mac, Mary Le Hair, Shirley Venables, Jane Wakerley, Jonathan Wakerley, Jane Matthews, Jenny Smith, Caroline Davies, Pedro, Brian Yates, Big Norm, Carol Doughty, Avis Hand, Jock Beaton, Paddy.

Nottingham:-

Susan Ward, Eileen Clayton, Alan Randall, Sheila Cater, Pete Lemon, Pee Wee, Knocker, Dusty, Sailor, Fuzz, George, Gray Whalley and the Mini Men, Celia, Cynthia, John Charity, Janice Elliot, Dave Cocking, June (and all the Sneinton girls), Mozz, Peter Wilson, Jenny Stanley, John Kirk, Seamus and the Henchmen, Chris Bowering, Randy, Phil Long, Chas Barlow, Barry Kendrick, Nigel Tatton, Maxine Foster, Ashley Grice, Stewpot, Nigel Dean, Pauline, Elaine Spray, Ken Burt, Stew Biddolph, Julian Foster, Russell Foster, Robo, Carol, Pip, Cupe, Stuart Cater, Pam Mullins., Gordon Long, Lol, Tony Soper, Maureen Rose, Carol, Gordon, Sonya Bohmer, Dave Whittle, Kevin Parks, Keith, John Rogers, Norman, Tong, Glen, Malc, Beverley, Jeanette, Alan Humphreys, Haydn Parmenter, Paul Smith, Sherrie Hutchinson.

Sutton in Ashfield/Mansfield/Chesterfield:-

Lard, Harry, Pop Jackson, Mick North, Dave Trogg.

Retford:

The two sisters (with dark hair)

Boston:

Pete Burt, Brenda and Margaret, and everyone from "The Copper Kettle".

Stamford/Castle Bytham:-

Nimrod Green, John Leddington, Dennis Allen, George Jarvis, Ann Allen , Annie and June Neal.

Lincoln:-

Larry Richards, The Duke, Pete, Beverley Brown.

Peterborough:

The Laughing Boy, The Soke Boys (and Girls)

Anybody who ever danced, drank or breakfasted, in the following clubs, pubs, cafés and dancehalls,:-

Dungeon, Nottingham
Face, Grantham
Mojo, Sheffield
Copper Kettle, Boston
Gliderdrome, Boston
Black Cat, Huddersfield
Twisted Wheel, Manchester
Barracks, Grantham
Bowling Green, Newark
Bass House, Skegness
Britannia, Nottingham
Boat, Nottingham
Union, Nottingham
Beachcomber, Nottingham
Clouds, Derby
Kardomah, Nottingham
Peep Hole, Leicester
Marco's, Grantham
Viking, Lincoln
Reindeer, Grantham
Royal Children, Nottingham
Sawyers Arms, Nottingham
Salutation, Nottingham

And also Edna, my mother, whom I must have led a merry dance in the 60s!

AF

*

THE NEW HORIZON

CAN I GET A WITNESS?

`Two Park Drive packets!'
`You what'
`You asked me what the gap was and I told you. I always gap it with two Park Drive packets.'
`Let's have a look.' Andy asked.
Don passed it up to Andy.
`It's all shitted up!' Andy said, studying the waste land of the plug's electrode. `When did you last clean it!'
`Dunno' Don remarked absently - `Boxing Day I think.'
Andy looked at the sky, in feigned disgust, as a grin cracked Don's face in two.

The machine to which the spark plug belonged was a Lambretta LI 150 Rally Master Motor Scooter. It was painted white with black and red horizontally striped side panels (one lay on the ground, exposing the engine's skeletal framework). Straddled across the front mudguard was a tubular chrome luggage rack, from which sprouted four mirrors and five spot-lamps on slim stalks of varying lengths. Numerous cotton and felt flags - emblems of England's coastal resorts - Skegness, Margate, Clacton and Yarmouth completed the livery.

The rear rack held a spare wheel, with its white-wall tyre, bolted on to the top rung. A fur covered backrest for the pillion passenger took support from the spare wheel it rested against. The word "NEWARK", written in white capital letters traced the perimeter of the small perspex fly screen fastened to the handlebars. In the mid 60s bikes such as this were ridden by a sector of English youth, known collectively as Mods.

Don was a Mod.
Like the majority of his contemporaries in this English sub-culture phenomenon (including Andy) much of Don's life was spent under his bike, in front of a mirror or on a dance floor.

Andy handed the plug back to Don, he was already folding the cigarette packet into his makeshift feeler gauge.
`Where're we going on the Bank Holiday Don?' Andy asked, returning his attention to the paper he had been reading. `The word is - Yarmouth.'

'Skeg.' Don was emphatic, snapping the HT lead firmly over the now shiny white porcelain of the spark plug. `Anybody who's anybody 'll be at Skeg - which naturally includes us!'
`Might be worth going to Boston on the Saturday, then on to Skeggy,' Andy said, scanning down the new Musical Express listings, `says here the Small Faces are playing at the Gliderdrome that night.'
`Yeah - pity it has to be Boston though - the place just crawls with grease - the bastards, hundreds of 'em, hang about outside just, waiting for you. Like that Who show last month.'
`Don't worry' Andy smiled - `Milt can sort 'em out, like he's always saying he will.'

Milt, their absent friend, was also a Mod.

Grease - AKA Motorcyclists. AKA Rockers (mainly by the out-crowd and journalists not quite close enough to the street). They wore black leather jackets peppered with studs, plastered their hair thick with Brylcreem and rode fast, noisy motorbikes with Americanoid names like Triumph Bonneville, BSA Goldstar, Indian Brave, Norton Dominator, Ariel Leader.

To Don, and their crowd they looked like something which had just crawled out of the 50s - that in itself was about as low as you could get in the tidal wave of 60s newness; the fact that greasers could travel faster in first gear than a Mod's scooter could move flat out mattered not. They may have been the true and logical face of post-war rebelliousness, remnants from another decade and it's rock 'n' roll - again it mattered not.

Sure, they had the speed - but no style.

Occasionally these two factions fought each other on the beaches and streets of designated seaside towns. Raw four-stroke power versus cultured two-stroke chic.

Don tinkered with his engine for another ten minutes or so while Andy, seated on Don's bike, his back against the rest and feet draped either side of the fly screen, idly thumbed through the paper.

` 'Say Don, do you mind if I ride with you when we go to Skeggy' Andy asked cagily, still reading.
`Why, what's wrong with your bike?' Don asked `Clapped out?'
` 'could piss yours in second.' Andy responded quickly to the jibe, but his tone changed just as speedily to the apologetic `No - I'm about skint - three payments behind on the bike and another two to make on my suit - I've gotta get that before the Bank Holiday.'
`You can for me.' Don answered, gathering up his tools and replacing the scooter's side panel.

`I don't want to sponge you know' Andy looked sheepish, `I feel like the bloke out of "Subterranean Homesick Blues" - need eleven dollar bills and I've only got ten.'
'Forget it! - when I've got it we can spend it - when I ain't, we can't - 'simple as that. Right.'
`Right.' said Andy, relieved, and quickly changed the subject - `Start her up.'
Don grinned, bent under the back of Andy's knees and turned the petrol tap on, `Mind your arse then.'
Andy climbed off the seat and stood back a couple of paces as Don grabbed the throttle grip and forced the kick start to the floor with his right foot. The engine fired first time. The pair of them grinned, took heart from the sound of the engine as Don opened and closed the throttle.

'Sounds good,' Andy said `bit smoky though.' pointing at the colour of the exhaust.
`No problem,' said Don - `half a turn on the mixture 'll sort it.' As he yanked the twist grip downwards the engine roared again and a face appeared at the upstairs window of the neighbouring house.

`Shut that racket off!' shouted the hairnet from number 46 - `My husband's trying to sleep!'
` 'not surprised - 'state of you.' Andy muttered, looking to Don for endorsement.
`You know he's on nights. You've got no consideration!'
`Consideration!' Don retorted angrily. ` 'that what you call it when your kids use my old man's chrysanths for target practice - prat!'

`Now listen Donald. Don't you start mouthing .....'

`Sorry - can't hear you.' Don grinned at Andy, yanking the throttle back again and again. The Lambretta's engine note at 5000 rpm was enough to convince the woman that further protest was futile. She slammed the window shut. All Don and Andy could do was to lip read the woman's rantings.

Don killed the engine and turned to Andy laughing. `Do you wanna lift home!'
`No you're OK - I'll walk. I'll cut through the school.'
`Right - I'm just going to wash her - see you at the Castle.'
` 'bout half-seven, yeah?' Andy picked up his paper and walked off down the road.
`Half-seven.' Don confirmed with his thumb and went to fetch his sponge and bucket.

*

By the time Don was rinsing the last of the suds off the Lambretta Andy had reached the playing field of his old school. He peeled back the loose chain link fencing in the corner of the field, gaining access to the shortcut he had used for years. As he walked across the grass towards the buildings the memories of those years came flooding back - double Latin on Thursday afternoons, the enforced playing of Shinty when the ground was too frozen for Rugby, the pliant sarcasm of the Physics Master and the uncontrollable violence of "Cod's Eye", the English Teacher. He grimaced at the recovered sight of the blood smeared over the forehead of one of his form mates, who'd been laid unconscious by a board rubber, thrown with inch perfect accuracy by this particular master, from his desk's raised dais, to the back of the class. "Cod's Eye" always boasted of his prowess at fielding and the number of "run outs" he had notched up in the cricket playing days of his youth - how he could have played for Notts., if he'd had the chances.

The majority of the school kids wished he had.

Andy approached the back of the Chemistry Lab, deserted now for the school holidays. It all seemed like another planet. The buildings, strong, silent, aged as they were, appeared to him as transcient as the sunlight which warmed their brickwork and brought small beads of sweat to his forehead. Oh, how he couldn't wait to leave this school. His last year had seemed like eons. While his former schoolmates were laying down the foundations for their last two years in the 6th form and their eventual passage to university, Andy had swapped their lives of academia for another, as equally demanding but infinitely more exciting - the streets of the 60s.

As he passed through the front gates into the street he thought he was hearing the cries of his house team and its touchline supporters, watching his last rugby match.

Of the two youths, Andy was the thinker. This was not so much due to his time spent at grammar school, but probably because thought was free and Andy never seemed to have enough money. The education he had received, resulting in the clutch of `O' levels he had somehow managed to secure, was, at this time, almost totally wasted on him. On the other hand Don, whose rudimentary schooling had culminated in him completing the best part of his last school year as a truant, was never short of cash.

There was a moral here which Andy was currently trying to come to terms with.

*

Don was still lavishing attention on the prime example of his private material wealth, buffing up the last piece of polish from the Lambretta's front mudguard, when his mother emerged from the house and walked down the path to him. She looked agitated, upset.

'Her next door's been on again - about the noise of that thing.' Don's mother snapped.

`It's not a thing - it's a scooter. A bike.' Don retorted.

`We've got to live next door to her.'

`Yeah and don't we know it.' Don replied, still busy polishing.

`Anyway Donald I've just had Ivy on the phone. You know - Bert's next door neighbour.'

`We ain't got a phone.'

`She rang number 25,' she said indignantly `anyway let me tell you,' she went on. `Bert's died - sudden like. This morning - straight after the night-shift. Mavis'll be in a state.'

`Yeah, pissed out of her head from celebrating.' Don said, without looking up.

`Donald. Did you hear what I said! Bert's just died.'

`Yep I heard.' He said, looking up to his mother. `Do I clap or cry!'

`Now don't speak ill of the dead!'

`Dead or alive - he's still a bastard.' He returned to the beautification of the Lambretta's paintwork.

`That's a wicked thing to say.'

`But it's true. It makes me weep. Somebody like Bert, who everybody knows was bad news, goes and pegs it and folks start talking about him like he was a fuckin' saint!'

`I won't have talk like that !' his mother flushed, more from embarrassment than outrage.

`Well you ask our Mavis what she thinks about it then - he was a right bastard to her all his life.'

Mrs.Hadden pondered quietly. Her son Donald polished.

`Ivy says the funeral's on Saturday - funny day for a funeral. Must have had to arrange it special - probably had to pay extra. Mavis told me that he always said he wanted to be buried at 3 o'clock on a Saturday - kick off time. You know how he loved Notts. County ....' the voice was quiet, subdued. She seemed distant as she spoke.

Don started to laugh `Why not do a job lot - get a good discount and bury the team with him - might as well, 'way they've been playing lately.'

`You'll have to come to the funeral.' His mother said seriously.

`Will I?'

`It's only right.'

`When is it?'
`It's a week on Saturday.'
`No chance !'
`What do you mean?' his mother asked.
`I mean it's Bank Holiday - we're off to the coast.' He shook the duster and a shower of dried white particles of polish drifted to the ground between them.
`You'll have to come Don.'
`No chance !'
`You'd upset Mavis if you didn't go ....'
Don looked at his mother and she, sensing that she had momentarily pierced what the young regarded as natural indifference and their elders took for obstinacy, continued quickly - `you know how much she likes you - don't upset her.'
He ran his figures gently over the thin film of polish on the Lambretta's panel, looking almost through the bike. A temporary quietness settled on the street. Mrs. Hadden started to button her coat, preening reflectively.
`I really ought to pop down to Mavis's - see how things are - if she wants anything. Will you nip us down there on your thing?'
'It's not a bloody thing!'
`Well your motor bike - will you - please?'
`Oh God why!' Don said `can't you walk, or catch the bus - you look such a lulu on the back of me.'
`OK then,' the sigh was as deep as the Trent - `don't know how long it'll take me to get there.'
`Oh alright then,' Don capitulated and started to pack up his dusters and polishes - `only if you ride properly and stay still when I'm cornering.'

Don straddled the bike, started it up, selected the first gear and let the clutch out. The drive took up and the engine's power was transmitted to the wheel. Rubber gripped Tarmacadam and the scooter moved forward, its stand slamming up against the underside of the running boards. It would have been easier to push the bike off its stand. Easier - but less dramatic. Don revved the bike, listening discerningly to the note of the engine as his mother seated herself behind him. She put her arms around his waist for support.

`Now don't cling on to me like a Mole Grip,' he said, pushing her backwards towards the rest behind her, `I don't want to look a prat.'
Mrs. Hadden took a pleated rainhood from her handbag. Don turned around at the sound of the plastic, snap, crackling and popping, as she opened it.

`You're not wearing that!' he said in disbelief.

'It'll ruin my hair if I don't.' His mother pulled the hood over her head and fastened it tightly beneath her chin. With a look of resigned disgust Don and his mother moved off down the road in the same direction Andy had walked earlier.

*

If Andy had looked around as he was entering Barnby Gate he would have seen the familiar Lambretta flash by - piloted by Don, with his mother on the pillion seat, one hand firmly around her son's waist and the other clutching at her plastic rainhood, flapping wildly in the wind which howled around her now not-so-permanent wave.

Andy however, didn't look around. As he walked the last few hundred yards to his house his mind was elsewhere. He was busy thinking about the new suit he was due to collect next Friday. He smiled as he recalled his first visit to the John Collier Shop five or six weeks back to select the cloth and be measured for the garment. If Andy's choice of the bottle green gaberdine material hadn't been revelation enough for the bemused assistant then his precise instructions for the suit's styling were sufficient to challenge the man's traditional tailoring background to its limits - parallel trousers, semi-hipster cut, 15" bottoms, no pleats, cut close around his backside; the jacket, with wider lapels than the Italian styling, currently being worn by Everly Brothers look-alikes, would sport flapped pockets with a small ticket pocket on the left hand side, exactly 2½" above the larger one; it would be long, with a three button fastening, a shaped waist and a 17" centre vent slashed up the back.

The green cloth had been buried in the last of the swatch books that Andy had been shown. He had been through all the samples in the shop, much to the tried patience of the staff, whose proferring of pinstripes and Glen checks had all been lost on Andy, before he finally came across the dark green material and carressed it between his fingertips to confirm his choice. It had amused him when he had received a postcard from the shop a few days after his measuring up, saying that the factory had insisted on the rechecking of his choice of cloth and also the measurements and design of the suit. The material was still available the shop had confirmed, but the last time an order had been placed for it was in 1959 and would he call in to clarify. They went on to say that, in their considered opinion, the length of the centre vent in the jacket at 17" was excessive.

To Andy it was perfect - for in his mind he could see the jacket of the suit, swaying in time to the music in his head, as he danced away the night at

Skegness, a couple of weekends from now. The postcard had only served to confirm that his choice was kosher. This suit was important to him.

It would be different. It would get him noticed - and that was the nub of it. He had to get himself back into contention with his contempories. If you were a Mod in the 60s your clothes spoke volumes for you, and whilst, after a good night, he might stumble down the street, he wasn't prepared to **stutter** down it.

Don had recently taken a trip down to London and picked up a full length dark brown suede from some top class shop on Carnaby Street - (Andy could've killed for that coat) and Milt had bought himself a long red leather, when he and Andy had hitch-hiked up to Sheffield a couple of weekends ago. With this suit he would once again be on terms with his friends. As he approached the top of his street a thought came to mind of one of his mother's favourite adages - that "Manners Maketh Man." With his daydreams coated in a film of John Collier's bottle green gaberdine suiting he thought what a load of balls that often quoted phrase actually was.

Clothes, clothes, clothes, (not manners) maketh man.

He stopped outside the corner shop at the end of the street to tie his shoe lace and a middle aged man, neatly dressed, came out of a nearby door, which opened directly on to the street.

'Hello Andrew,' the man said.

Andy looked up to the voice and, ignoring the salutation, returned immediately to the task of his shoe lace. His finger nails tugged at a tight knot and kept him on his haunches.

`'ve you thought any more about my little proposition eh - just think what you could get - I saw you the other day looking at those white parallels in Masdins. They'd look good on you.'

Andy still fiddled with the knot in his lace, keeping his eyes on his shoe.

`And that Fred Perry - the one with the motif on the pocket,' the man went on, `oh you'd look so cool - think of the birds you could pull - you just come and see your Uncle Will .....'

Andy finally freed the tangled lace, re-tied the knot and rose abruptly.

`Oh just piss off !' he said sharply and walked away down the street.

`Think about it Andrew.' Will's words echoed as Andy entered the communal passage to his house. `You know where to find me .....'

*

Meanwhile, in another part of town a slim youth, stripped to the waist, was dragging a wash tub across the backyard of a terraced house. The soapy water in the tub spilled over the sides and seeped through the cracks in the paving to the earth beneath. Draped over his shoulders was a pair of blue denim jeans and dropping them into the soapy water he turned to the wash house nearby and fetched a wooden dolly punch from inside the door. More water slopped over from the tub, as the boy pounded the denim jeans ferociously. After a few minutes he stopped and turning from his labours, wiped the sweat which had formed on his forehead. A girl with short cropped hair had come into the yard a few minutes earlier and had been silently watching the boy. She smiled thinly as he became aware of her presence.
`Hello beautiful,' he said - `take yours off and I'll do 'em for you.' He grinned.
`No thanks Milt.' the girl's tone betrayed her uneasiness.
`Why not?' Milt urged - `got to get 'em just right - faded - 'reckon if I hung 'em up in the front room window it'd probably be quicker - bloody sun soon fades my old lady's curtains. Pass the bleach will ya?'

He pointed to the grate behind her. She handed him the bottle and he carefully poured a measured amount into the suds. Milt resumed the ponching process. The girl watched again, in silence, as Milt's arms rose and fell. The squelching sounds from within the tub punctuated the late afternoon. Water continued to spill over the yard as Milt pulled the jeans out from beneath the ponch and took them over to the wash house. The girl followed Milt inside, dodging the stream of soapy water dripping from the fabric.

An old iron, hand operated, mangle stood at the back of the wash house and Milt straightened his jeans out and fed them into the machine's Lignum wooden rollers. The girl moved over to Milt and brushing past him removed his fingers from the machine's handle and placed hers there instead. She started to turn it. Milt bent over and tried to kiss her. She turned her head away quickly and turned the handle faster.
`Hey careful Sharon - you'll crush the rivets.' He steadied her hand, his immediate concern centreing on the welfare of his Levis, rather than his spurned advances towards the girl.
`Milt, I've got to talk to you.' Sharon said softly, following him as he took the jeans from the mangle and went back into the yard. Milt either didn't hear or paid no attention and proceeded to fasten the wet jeans to the rear of a Vespa scooter, standing at the other end of the yard. He turned back to Sharon as he kick started the scooter's engine.

`'reckon a couple of laps around town 'll soon dry 'em.' He said, hoisting himself on to the front of the Vespa's seat. He revved the engine wildly as Sharon walked over to him.
`Milt I've got to talk to you .... '
`You 're talking to me.' He said, smiling at the sound of the engine as it echoed around the yard.
`I'm pregnant.'

His face dropped with the lowering of the engine's note.

`Since when?'
`Oh, I suppose since one Thursday night a couple of months back ....'
`You prat, how'd you manage that?' As soon as he'd spoken he wished he'd kept his mouth shut.
`Oh it's quite simple.' Sharon said, her voice starting to break up. `You just accept some good-looking boy's invitation to come round when his parents are away and then you take all your clothes off and .....' The tears then started to flow.
`Jesus! Jesus!' he said. Words repeated to buy time to deal with what he was being forced to contemplate. `Hey Sharon, I'll see you in a bit.' There was an instant, if only temporary solution, `I've got to get these jeans dry.' With these parting words he rode off down the passage into the street, still bare to the waist, with a pair of damp denim jeans flapping behind him. He banked the Vespa over, turned the corner and disappeared from his street. Sharon stood, her face in her hands, sobbing. Water in her eyes, water in the yard, strewn with spanners, cleaning rags and a half empty wash tub.

Milt's mother came out from the house and greeted the girl. `Hello Sharon - where's he gone then?'

`I don't know.' She swallowed hard and wiped her eyes quickly.
`Just look at this mess - just like him - never tidies anything up - wear the old ones out first.' Mrs.Milton picked up the bleach. `That's his motto - just like him - he didn't take you then?'
`No he didn't.'
`'you alright luv?'

***

OUT IN THE STREET

Don and Andy were draped over the steel railings outside the Castle, idly looking at the traffic which passed between them and the Ossington opposite and moved sluggishly behind them, along the old Fosse. Don had picked Andy up on his scooter and the early part of the evening had been spent aimlessly riding around the narrow streets of the town, in what amounted to a mobile advertising campaign.

There was a particular style in which a scooter was ridden in a built up area or indeed anywhere where a Mod had an audience. The pilot of the machine sat on the very front edge of the seat, with his knees touching the inside of the front boards. The feet were wedged in the angle where the front boards bent round to form the floor, with toes pointing downwards at an angle of exactly 45° to the horizontal.

The person who rode pillion stretched his legs out, straight under those of his companion and leaned into the back rest. His body formed an angle exactly 45° to the vertical. His arms were either clasped tightly behind his head or folded across his chest, presiding over the streets they passed through. Don and Andy had adapted and perfected this style, having first seen a version of it practised by some London Mods at Yarmouth, earlier in the year. The narrow streets of Newark and its shop windows provided an ideal way of checking their aesthetics.

Their favourite preening ground in this respect consisted of the western side of the cobbled market square running down into Stodman Street. It was here that the combined frontages of Marks & Spencer, Woolworths, John Collier and Harstons Music Shop, flanked by Montague Burton, part way on the right, provided them with a personal vanity mirror - some 60 yards long and 15 feet high.

The drone of traffic was incessant in this early part of the evening; caravans heading off to the east cost and local inhabitants heading for Nottingham in search of some brighter lights. Apart from watching traffic the pair of them were engaged in what had, of late, become a pastime, equally as boring and just as unwelcome - waiting for Milt.

`Where're we off tomorrow?' Andy said.
`Anywhere, anywhere.' Don replied. `Anywhere but here.'
'"The Mojo"?'
`Don't fancy Stringfellow's crowd .... do you?'
`Nah - not really.' Andy sighed and turned to Don. `Hey you 're seeing Sally, aren't you?'
`Nope !'
`Finished?' Andy enquired.
`Finished.' It was confirmed. `Wedding bells !'
`Not another?' Andy smiled.
`I'm irresistible - just can't help it.' Don grinned, but meant it. `She wanted me to meet her ma! - well!' Don turned to Andy `'you seeing anybody?'
`Not tomorrow.' Andy replied.
`Nobody 'd have you !'
`Bollocks !'
`We could go up to "The Wheel".' Don changed the subject and started singing `Oh Manchester, Manchester, Manchester United !'
`You could.' Andy said curtly. `I'm broke - you know.'
`When you gonna get yourself a proper job?' Don said dismissively.
`I've got one !'
`Have you bollocks ! - with what they pay you I don't know how you make out.'
'No - but when I've done my time .....' Andy went on, but was quickly interrupted.
`Then you 'll be too old to enjoy it - listen, I can get you on at the station if you want.'
`Oh I dunno - my old man says you've gotta do your time. Finish your apprenticeship.'
`Oh yeah. 's fine for him to spout, but he's not skint by Saturday dinner is he?'

The temporary silence which followed only served to confirm the weight of Don's words. Andy had always thought that the system was set up the wrong way round. He thought that you ought to be paid more when you were young, when you needed the money for clothes, petrol etc etc and then get less as you got older - he couldn't remember the last time his dad had bought any clothes or actually went anywhere.

`We could go to "The Face" on Sunday - Grantham's only 15 miles away - you could just about manage that !' The pair laughed at Andy's financial plight.
`Marco's 've got a disco on tomorrow. We could have the pick,' Andy said, 'we could stay over at Paula's.'

Don shrugged and then craned his neck and looked at the time on the clock tower of the factory on the opposite bank of the Trent, next to the bridge. `What time's Milt coming?' he asked.
`When he gets here. Andy replied. `I bet he's painting his bike or something....'

At that point their attention was drawn to the screech of a car's brakes in front of the Castle as the vehicle skidded to a stop to allow a Vespa motor scooter usurp its right of way. There were sparks coming from underneath as the magneto casing scraped the tarmac - so severe was the angle at which the bike had taken the corner. A few seconds later the scooter was parked on the cobble stones next to Don's, its rider unbuttoning his Parka.

`Milt,' Andy said disgustedly `you ride like a lunatic !'
`Andy, you say the nicest things.' Milt smiled back, draping his Parka over the railings. Don moved across to the side of Milt's bike for pit inspection. He bent beside the front of it and put his hand out towards the chrome rack.

`Hey ! don't touch the mudguard. It's still wet !'
`What d 'I tell you Don !' Andy shrieked.
`We're thinking of staying out tomorrow night Milt,' Don said. ` 'you game?'
`Why, is there a party or something?' Milt asked.
`Might be one we could crash,' Andy said `but I reckon we should go to Grantham - Marco's.'
`Oh yeah,' Milt said, pointedly `because a certain lady's given the lad a promise.'
`No, 's not that.' was Andy's sheepish reply.
`I tell you Andy,' Milt said with conviction `she's already doled out promises to half of Lincolnshire - and the other half 've already been there !'

The three laughed together. They had sex on the brain - permanently.
They fussed around their scooters (adjusting mirrors, repositioning spot-lights, wiping away the odd smear on the paint and chrome work) in between their traffic watching. This was interrupted presently as Milt leapt on to the middle rung of the iron railings, towering above the other two and waving two fingers at a noisy procession of leather clad motor cyclists, negotiating the roundabout, on their way towards Lincoln. `Bastards - greasers !' Milt shouted after the motorbikes.
`They're long gone Milt.' Don said drily. `Save it for the Bank Holiday. There'll be grease enough at Skeg... '

Milt was still standing on the railings as the line of traffic came to a halt, depositing, immediately in front of them, a Triumph Spitfire with its hood down.

A long blonde haired girl reclined in the passenger seat. Copious amounts of knee and thigh were revealed by the girl's short skirt, which had ridden up almost to her crotch. The car's seat belt pulled tightly across her chest, parting and emphasising the shape of her breasts, which were already more than amply defined by the tight, pink, skinny ribbed sweater she was wearing. She had a pair of large dark sun-glasses on and if she was aware of the three Mods gazing into the footwell of the car, she did not acknowledge it, keeping her eyes fixed firmly on the road, one hand tapping the side of the door in tune to the music which was coming out of the radio. The fingers of her other hand were absently flicking her long hair from her shoulders.

`Jeez I could give her one.' Don said, as the jam freed itself and the car moved off with the rest of the traffic.

`She's certainly a looker.' Milt said, drooling after the car as it disappeared.

`What's she doing with a prick like him?' Don bemoaned.

`Money.' Andy said, 'It has to be money - I used to go to school with him. You know - Simmonds The Builders. His dad owns it - he's the local hero to my old man - self-made man - all I get is how he dragged himself up - started off by building rabbit hutches. Now he's in the big time - house building....'

`We've got a contract painting his estate at Coddington.' Milt quipped, 'He still builds rabbit hutches - believe me!'

`Well I could still see to his lady.' Don drooled, the laughter of Andy and Milt going way over his head.

His drooling was curtailed by a tap on his shoulder from behind. A girl, with close cropped black hair and eyes heavy with mascara, smiled and addressed all three of them, who turned to her greeting, `What are you lot doing in town on a Friday night?'

`Seeing how the other half live.' Don smiled.

`Whose cow'd you kill Maggie?' Milt said, eyeing the full length maroon suede coat the girl was wearing. Don had walked behind the girl and putting his hand on each of her shoulders, slowly caressed the soft, yielding fabric of the coat, working his way down under her arms, brushing the outside of her breasts. He stopped with his arms around her waist. `Very smooth.' He said.

`Where's it from Maggie?' Andy joined in the conversation.

`Portobello Road.'

`Mm,' Don said, `when'd you go?'

`Last week-end - Phil took me.'

`Who's Phil?' Andy asked.

`He's from Peterborough ...'

`Not one of the Posh Boys?' Milt sounded disgusted.

`He knows them,' Maggie said, `but he's got a mini-van. Him and his mates say that some of the London crowd're making it pretty big in tarted up mini-vans....'
`Load of balls Maggie.' Milt was still disgusted.
`What's he like?' Andy asked.
`Mod. Very Mod.' she said.
`Maggie, I'm surprised at you.' Milt said.
`Does he know "The Smiler"?'
`Who doesn't know "The Smiler".' she answered quickly.
`The Posh.' Andy said. `50 miles down the A1 and they think they're Londoners!'.
`Yeah. Load of greasers !' said Milt.
`Nothing to stop us flashing down "The Smoke" is there fellahs?' Don said confidently.
`Any time man.' Milt confirmed.
`Nope - nothing at all,' Andy seconded it, but quickly added an after thought, `apart from the petrol money.'
`Where're you going tomorrow night?' Don asked her.
There's an all nighter at "The Wheel" - Phil's taking me.'
`Jeez, he must have some bread.' Andy commented.
`A little.' she replied, cagily.
`Where's he work Maggie?'
`He - er, works for himself.' Maggie replied to Don's question.
`Doing what?' Andy quizzed.
`Well - dealing....' she replied.
`Pill pushing.' Don elaborated for her.
`No. No - he deals in all sorts - equipment, clothes - you know.'

`Yeah, I know Maggie. I heard about him and his fucking crowd. Instead of dancing they're busy lifting back racks and anything else that glitters, on any body else's bike. The bastard had a caravan full of leathers a couple of weeks back at Yarmouth - all rolled.' Milt was animated `But I'd tell him if I was you Maggie - tell him, and his mates, including "The Smiler", that they'd better keep an eye over their shoulders....'
`Why's that Milt?' Maggie asked sarcastically.

`Because,' said Milt `because the word is that the Nottingham boys are pissed off with 'em and they're gonna wipe 'em out. The Sutton scooter lads 're already missing half their chrome !'
`Well I'd better tell him then, hadn't I - can't say he'll take a deal of notice though.... Hey, I'd better go.' She said, looking at her watch `I'm late, don't be too good.'

The three of them bade Maggie goodbye and watched, as her Hush Puppied feet carried her out of sight. They started to discuss her as soon as she was out of earshot. They had sex on the brain - permanently.
`'s a pity about the company she keeps 'cos I could make it with her!' Milt said and whistled through his teeth.
`I have.' Don smiled, `Three times.'
`You bugger - when?' Milt asked.
`Secret.' Don smiled.
`I've changed my mind.' Milt said, laughing `'wouldn't want to follow you - you creep.' He turned to Andy who had studiously avoided the conversation. `You're quiet Andy - don't tell me you've got a secret as well?'
Andy said nothing.

`And talking of which,' Milt continued `I saw Patti last night - and she still loves you.'
`'ve you made it yet?' Don joined in the conversation.

Andy walked round to Milt's scooter, in an attempt to divert the conversation elsewhere. `It's private.' He said, without looking at the others.
`Is it bollocks !' Don said.
`Well, have you?' Milt said quickly.
`I might have.' Andy replied.
`And you might not have.' Milt quipped.
`You know Andy, that lady's just aching for you. You can smell it. She's dying for you - 'reckon you need a couple of squirts of Redex.'
`Milt, piss off.' Andy shouted.
`Could be right Milt,' Don added.
`You bet I'm right,' Milt spoke with authority, `that's the trouble with you grammar school tykes. Too busy reading poetry and all that stuff - send her round to me. I'd help you out.' He finished his mini speech by making a fist of his left hand and clenching the biceps, thrust his arm skywards.

Andy was uncomfortable at the attention currently being focused on him and once more tried to remove himself from the centre of the conversation. `When did you last see Sharon, Milt?' Andy asked. The painful reality of his relationship with Sharon came home to Milt, as Andy's casual question recalled the events in his backyard earlier in the day. Events he had been studiously ignoring, in the naive hope that they would go away.
`Oh, a couple of days ago,' he lied, `it's no big deal.'
`Hey Milt,' Don asked, smiling `when was your last time?'

`I made it with one of them Stamford bints behind "The Barracks" at Grantham last Saturday.' Milt answered, eager to blot out temporarily all thoughts of Sharon and their joint problem.
`And what about you Andy?' Don quizzed Andy, who could feel his neck and face reddening.
`Dunno.' he said, trying to be nonchalant ` 'don't keep track.'
`Say, Andy,' Milt said, `have you ever done it?'

Andy was mortified. His throat dried up, he swallowed hard, searching desperately for saliva. After those few lapsed seconds Don dived in.
` You haven't, have you?' Don's tone was almost paternal (sympathetic?).
`Well I've nearly.' Andy blurted out quickly, defensively (apologetically?).

The mood changed dramatically from one of curiosity to hilarity. Don and Milt ended up draped over the railings, totally convulsed and helpless with laughter. Andy looked round for a hole he could quietly crawl into. All he was able to do was to watch the tears roll down the cheeks of his friends and re-live some pertinent moments of his immediate past.

(He had, over the past couple of months, nearly lost his virginity three times. On one occasion, after picking up a girl from Strelley at "The Dungeon" in Nottingham, they were in danger of doing it at the back of the Mount Street Bus Station, when her last bus arrived. He was beset by a similar set of frustrating circumstances in a drafty passage way, when he was deep into the underwear of a girl from Balderton and her dad, returning home, had prevented further progress in any direction.

He still possessed the bruises - and the scars made by his zip.
The last time had been with a girl, who was, it transpired, also a virgin but at the very last moment had decided that actually she wanted to do it with Don for her first time... the bastard!)

Eventually some sort of sanity prevailed. Milt and Don composed themselves.
`Hey Don,' Milt said, wiping the tears from his eyes `this is serious,' and, turning to Andy, `you can't keep it hid all your life Andy. It ain't natural.'
`You can pull something at Skeg and see to it.' Don kept up the pressure, `And woe betide you if you don't - can't keep it shrinked wrapped forever, eh Milt?'
'Right !' said Milt and turned to Andy, `'you all fixed up?'
`What with?' Andy looked puzzled.
`Spivveys you prat.' Milt said. Andy shook his head.
`OK then.' Don said, putting on his Parka and pointing towards the rear seat of the Lambretta. `Let's go.'
Andy was still puzzled. `Where to?'

Milt was already astride his bike, revving it. `The barber's - Smithies are open 'til half eight.'
` I don't need a haircut.' Andy said, as Don kicked his bike into life.
`Now what do you get from the barber's - apart from haircuts?' Milt said in the manner of a school teacher.
`Shaving cream?' Andy smiled.
`Spivveys you prat ! Don repeated Milt's words and Andy was slammed into the back rest, as the scooter moved off from the Castle. Milt followed them and they rode across town, weaving through the traffic. Don stopped outside the barber's shop and gently pushed Andy off the pillion. `Well go on then.' Milt, still astride his bike, looked on grinning widely. Andy turned, said nothing, but pulled both his pockets inside out - Billy Bunter style. Don handed him a couple of two shilling pieces and watched as Andy walked slowly into the barber's shop.

He came out shortly, there was an air of embarrassment about him.
`Well, what sort d' you get then?' Don said, prising Andy's fingers from around the package in his hand.
`Gillettes.' Andy said. They all looked at the razor blades in the palm of Andy's hand. With a flourish Don took the blades and the change from the transaction and, having dug into his pocket, thrust a packet of Durex into Andy's hand.
`Now get stuck in !' Don admonished. Milt shook his head and smiled.

Andy nodded silently in agreement.

*

It was nearly 11.00 pm by the time Andy was letting himself into his house. His parents had gone to bed; for them the weekend had started an hour earlier than the TV programme which was now being broadcast by Rediffusion into the living rooms of a large section of the nation.

Andy turned on the TV set and twiddled the tuning dial - the organised chaos of "Ready Steady Go!" materialised in front of him - literally hundreds of kids (mainly Mods) being pushed around the studio floor by camera and floor crew as they fought for their positions to film the acts, who were, in the main, indistinguishable from the audience and at the same level on the floor of the studio.

This was a show where the audience mixed it with the stars who, unashamedly, mimed their way through their songs, mouths usually a bar or two behind the record. There were few raised stages for the artists to perform on - there might be the occasional use of a scaffolding tower or a spiral staircase but in the main it was shoulder rubbing, foot stamping, B.O. swapping, audience participative mayhem. Part of tonight's show, however, featured one of their more spectacular sets and Andy watched the cameras zoom in onto a flight of open steps, which swooped down to a stage in the middle of the floor. The Mods surrounded the raised dais. Andy gazed spellbound and breathless, as a tiny girl, with hair bobbed at shoulder length, framing an oval face, ran down the stairs, onto the stage. She was wearing a tight sweater and light coloured, close fitting hipster jeans, which hugged her calves and thighs, her hips thrusting provocatively as she started to sing.

Shout ! Shout ! Shout ! Shout !

She sang wildly. The studio audience shook with frenzy - Andy could see daylight between her thighs, as the tight fabric formed a horse shoe shape either side of her crotch. He was totally wiped out by the raw energy the girl pumped out, unable to take his eyes off her, as she screamed out the song.

He had read about varying styles of song delivery in one of the rock music papers recently - but it had all been the usual pseudo intellectual rubbish, garnished with over the top of his head jargon - the stuff of the lit.crit. he had baulked at during his schooldays. All mind numbing journalistic clamour; proffering explanations of the social relevances of Dylan's peculiar emphasis on rhyme and phrasing?!? - the outrageous chords of the Beatles reduced to the level of a matriculation board exam?!? - the cultured sneering of Jagger as political posturing?!? - he had read of The Who's violent instrument smashing stage act - the journalist describing it as Auto-Destructive Art! The sophistication of Sinatra's microphone technique had been referred to as a metaphor for the American dream ! Such crap, he thought. But, what he was now seeing on the television screen was to Andy so direct, so vital, it defied description.

It just **was**.

The girl didn't even look like the Mod girls he hung around with, but it didn't matter. Her performance had a purity about it, an indefinable quality - all the Shakespearean sonnets, the Elizabethan love poetry, the muse of French Symbolism, with which he had been force fed at school, paled into insignificance when confronted with the two and a half minutes of this song.

The science of a song's delivery? Balls he thought. Balls! Forget it man. She was screwing the song - straight into his head, screwing it to to the sticking-place - here in his front room.

It was that simple.

The fact that she was being watched by a couple of million others was immaterial. He felt it was only reaching his ears and eyes.

Shout ! Shout ! Shout !

This, for him, had a sexual significance, which transcended the mores of pop music and its accessibility. This liberated the lust in him. This was personal.
He went to sleep shattered, clutching the packet of contraceptives and with a head full of confusing and contradictory thoughts. All placed there by Marie McDonald Lawrie - Lulu.

*

In the week that led up to the Bank Holiday Andy was no nearer fulfilling his role as lover of all women, but he had made the last thirty shilling payment on his suit and now it was his. He was well pleased with the way it had turned out. The silky lining to the jacket made it glide over his torso when he had danced all the way home from John Collier's, still wearing it.

On the Saturday morning he was alone in Newark town's centre. Don and Milt were busy tarting their bikes up for the Bank Holiday weekend. They were leaving for the coast in the afternoon. He had managed to save a couple of pounds from his last few week's wages and had been scouring the town for a new T shirt, to complement his suit. He had found nothing remotely like the vision in his mind's eye. He should have gone to Nottingham and checked out Jeff's or the Birdcage, but there was no time (nor the money) for that.

He turned in desperation to Ricks Outfitters shop on the cobble stone market place. Although not particularly noted for its dedication to fashion, Ricks had been the place where his first long trousered two piece suit had been bought for him when he was thirteen and he was just playing a hunch. A sentimental hunch probably.

`You wouldn't have a white three button T shirt with, black stripes down one side would you?' Andy asked the man in the shop after their initial salutation.
`Not with black stripes,' the man shook his head. `I don't get much call for stripes nowadays.'

Andy was stumped, but cast his eye around the shop; a traditional tailors, with only the slightest leaning to what was happening, fashion wise, in the street. His eyes lit up like a pinball machine as he pointed to a garment, arranged carefully on a chest and shoulders dummy, tucked away in the corner of the window.
`How much is that Fred Perry in the window?'
`The one with the waggly tail?' Mr Rick joked. Andy warmed to the unhurried atmosphere of the shop and the easy mirth of its keeper. The place buzzed with the ring of their shared laughter. The ambience of the shop, with its polished wooden floors and oak panelling, would have differed markedly from its time in the Civil War when, in 1645, as the plaque on the wall outside recorded, Prince

Rupert had stayed in the building after his quarrel with the King.
`How much?' Andy asked again.
`Twenty seven & sixpence - do you want it?' Mr Rick asked him.
`If it fits.' said Andy.
Andy emerged from the fitting room wearing the Fred Perry. It fitted perfectly.
`I'll take it please.' he said.
`But it hasn't got stripes.'
`It will have.' said Andy, completing the purchase with a handful of silver coins.

His last stop before setting off for home was Currys, in the opposite corner of the market place. He came out of that shop with a brown paper bag containing a roll of shiny black insulation tape.

*

Andy was in his bedroom in front of the mirror. There was a pair of scissors on the dressing table and cut lengths of the black insulation tape were draped carefully over the glass topped Lloyd Loom linen basket. He smiled inwardly at his resourcefulness and his blueprint for a white T shirt, with a home made facility for an indefinite number of black striped patterns thereon - horizontal, diagonal, vertical, chevrons. The possibilities were endless. Necessity, in Andy's case, being the grandmother of invention.

He was peeling one of the lengths of tape from his chest when his mother entered the bedroom.
`'been buying again Andy?' she said, seeing the bags strewn on the bed.
`Nothing much.' he said, moving in front of the linen basket in an attempt to conceal its display of insulation tape.
`Let's have a look then.' she said, moving towards him.

`It's only a T shirt.' he said, folding his arms over his chest, as if the scrutiny of someone aged over twenty might alter its molecular structure. His mother looked hurt but quickly concealed her feelings.
`I've been buying as well,' she said, delving into the carrier bag she was holding. `I got my Co-op divi - I've bought you a present.'
Andy looked on apprehensively as his mother pulled a dark brown woollen cardigan from the bag. It had large "football" leather buttons and was as far as far could be from anything he'd wear. He tried to disguise his horror of the thing.

`Here, do you like it?' his mother asked, thrusting the cardigan towards him. He took it betwen his forefinger and thumb, holding it away from his body, with his arm outstretched, as if it was diseased and contagious.
`It's ... it's very nice.' he said unconvincingly.
`His mother sensed his true feelings towards her purchase. `You don't like it do you?' She was hurt.
`It's OK .' he said.
`You don't like it.' She confirmed for herself.
`No, it's fine, really.' he replied.
`You don't have to lie.' his mother said sharply.
`Look - I've told you before not to buy me clothes !'
`Well, it's the last thing you'll get from me.'
`Thank God.' he muttered under his breath (or as he thought).
`You ungrateful little sod !' his mother retaliated.
`I do appreciate it ma - honestly - but...'
`But nothing,' his mother said, `well you've done it with me - just because it's not like the rest of the tat in your wardrobe.'
`Ma, they're not wearing stuff like that...'
`They? - who's they?' she interrupted.
`The kids, my mates.' he tried to explain.
`And I suppose if they all put their heads in the gas oven or jumped in the Trent then you'd follow them, eh?' Her observation was logical... and true.
`Ma. You just don't see it... it's not that... it's.... God, you just don't see it. I can't wear it. I can't !'
`Well that's it.' she said coldly. `You've done your day with me. I buy you something and you throw it back in my face.' She snatched the cardigan from him and stormed out of the bedroom. He called after her but the only response he got was the slamming of the door at the bottom of the stairs. He stood and looked in the mirror. For a brief time he hated himself. Hated how the conversation had veered out of control; but deep in his head he knew the last few minutes couldn't have turned out any other way. He either moved in the direction of his peers or was moved aside.

He turned on his transistor radio and the faint signal from Radio 270, the pirate ship moored just off the Scarborough coast, crackled through the speakers. Robert Snyder, one of his friends at school, was a DJ on this pirate station. The strident chords of The Who's "Can't Explain" drifted in and out of his ears on the station's erratic signal.

He turned back to his "do it yourself" striping kit, experimenting with some more design combinations. He really couldn't explain. He listened to the radio

while messing around with the T shirt until his activity was curtailed by his father's entrance to the bedroom. Andy turned the radio off, knowing full well what to expect.
`Just what the hell do you think you're doing?' his father shouted.
`Just messing around.' said Andy vaguely.
`Is that what you were doing when you upset your mother - messing around!'
`I can't wear it dad.' he said emphatically but calmly.
`No, you'd sooner wear stuff like that.' his dad said, pointing to Andy's T shirt. `Bloody crazy if you ask me.'
`Well I didn't.'
`Now you can cut that out ! Mr Findern retorted angrily `Where's your bloody respect, Christ, when I was a kid my dad would 've skinned me for just looking at him in that tone of voice. When I think of what we've done for you, putting you through Grammar School, encouraging you with your homework... you get your "0" levels and what's it taught you eh?... how to upset your mother and stick insulation tape on a bloody tennis shirt !..... Christ, I wonder sometimes.'
`I didn't upset her on purpose.' Andy defended himself. `I've told her before not to buy me clothes. She doesn't know what we're wearing.'
`And it's not surprising she doesn't is it eh, when you buy your outfits from Currys ! Next thing'll be a bloody Hoover pipe for a scarf !' Mr Findern snatched the end of one of the pieces of insulation tape and ripped it from Andy's chest.

`God, don't carry on about school.' Andy snatched the tape back, `And work's just the same... OK, I got seven "0" levels but I don't earn a quarter as much as Don, do I?... and he spent half his life legging it off school down the billiard hall. So you tell me who's the prat - him or me? He says he can get me a job at the Power Station, with enough money to burn.'
`And how long do you think that 'll last eh? ... that just about sums your lot up.' His dad ranted on `You can't see further than the weekend... it's things like that "Ready Steady Go!" programme that's done it. They ought to be bloody prosecuted.... I mean the people that's making this country great - like John Bloom, Cyril Lord - the grafters... they don't spend their time listening to Cathy McGovern or Monkey dancing all night. They get a trade and stick to it. You've got to get a trade Andy and keep it.'

`But I don't earn enough money.' Andy protested.
`You'll get the big money... when you've done your time.' his dad said.

`'sounds like a prison sentence. Dad, I'm talking about **now**, when I need money. Now! Not in ten years' time.'
`I tell you that Cathy McGovern's responsible.' Mr Findern shook his head in disbelief. `Her and them Rolling Stones - peeing in the streets, dirty sods !'
'But I want a proper wage. Now ! I mean I'm gonna look a right burk if I ever make it to sixty five and then can just about afford to shell out on a new Lambretta GT 200. I can just see me - grey hair, stoned out of my head on Phyllosan, fur on my Parka coming out, haring down London Road croaking "My Generation" ... yeah ! Great. Anyway I'm thinking of packing it in....'
`Packing what in?' his father rounded on him.
`The job.' Andy said coolly.'
`We'll see about that !'

* * *

The Coast

Catch the Wind

It was the kind of afternoon that only an English summer could provide. Blue and brilliant.

I am the resurrection and the life.

Andy and Milt were basking in the heat. Both were lying horizontally on the scooters, with their feet dangling over the handlebars. Milt was reclined across his Vespa, Andy was draped over Don's Lambretta. A tightly rolled sleeping bag was fastened to the front rack of Milt's bike. Don's scooter had sleeping bags on both front and rear carriers. Andy was wearing his new green suit and white T shirt, the black stripes thereon softening in the sun. The jeans which Milt had been soaking and bleaching all through the week clung snugly to his legs, complemented by a new pair of beige desert boots.

For we brought nothing into this world and it is certain we can carry nothing out.

Three khaki coloured army Parkas were hanging from the black iron railings which topped the low wall nearby. The hoods of all three Parkas were trimmed with fur. Don's had a set of sergeant's stripes sewn on to the left shoulder. Milt's had a small circular tear in the fabric below the seam of the sleeve. He swore it was a bullet hole. There was a cloth badge on Andy's coat at breast height, embroidered with the words "U.S. Army".

Naked came I out of my mother's womb and naked shall I return thither.

' 'that your new suit?' Milt asked Andy, his eyes closed, enjoying the sun. 'Picked it up from Colliers on Friday.' Andy confirmed.

'Looks like you've still got the coat hanger in it.' Milt remarked casually. 'Balls!' Andy knew when Milt was joking - or thought he did. He knew this suit conferred status on him. Skegness would be a catwalk.

Yea, though I walk through the valley of the shadow of death.

The solemn ritual of Bert's funeral was perpetrated in the protocol of the procession which filed quietly from the graveside - with the exception of Don. He walked behind the rest of the mourners and (unlike his arrival) didn't leave in the first car. He came out of the cemetery as the last of the cortège was disappearing into the haze of the afternoon. He took his Parka from its temporary peg on the railings of the cemetery wall and tapped Andy on the shoulder.
'Let's ride.' he said, pulling on his Parka.
'Good funeral?' Milt said, raising himself.
Don said nothing. Andy got up and put on his Parka. Milt pulled a pair of sun glasses, with chromium coated lenses, from his pocket, cleaned them with a combination of spit and sleeve and hooked them around his ears. He turned his head sideways in both directions, checking out his newly diffused vision of the world.'
'What's with the disguise Milt?' Andy said, 'Who're you trying to avoid?'
'That raver from Sheffield I bet.' Don said, already starting to thaw from the coolness of the funeral. He started the Lambretta's engine.
'God, if she's there I'll turn grease and buy me a crash hat.' There was a despair in Milt's tone. He turned on the Vespa's petrol tap and the engine note matched that of Don's bike as it responded to the kick start.

The Fosse, which 2000 years earlier had echoed with the slap of leather on its metal, as the legions marched northwards, now carried soldiers of a new order. The road took them through Lincoln and the Stonebow Roman arch, high above the flood meadows of the Witham and out into the shire. They branched off eastwards, their route whisking them through Wragby and Horncastle. In a couple of hours they could see the concrete water towers of the coastal town and taste the salt in the air. Throughout the journey Andy leaned back into the rest, watching Lincolnshire unfold its sprawling fields before him. In his head he sung the words of his version of the song:

It winds up from Seaton in the south,
Right through to Grimsby, way past Louth
Get your kicks
On the A46.

They had met Mods coming down from Yorkshire and Grimsby, south from the Fens and Peterborough, coasting in on a mixture of India rubber and rhythm 'n' blues.

Chrome horses and diplomats.

Their two scooters formed part of a chrome cavalcade by the time they turned left at the Clock Tower and filed along the Prom past the "Jolly Fisherman" pub and the rows of cafés and guest houses. The advertising hoarding on the pier thrust onto the street the face of its present incumbent for the season.

Dickie Valentine was not a Mod.

They cruised around the town, which looked on with a sense of outrage, tinged with trepidation as to how the weekend would unfold, with its acquisition of this temporary khaki clad population.

There was already a noticeable police presence.

The three of them eventually peeled off from the convoy and parked the bikes in a yard formed by the backs of three buildings, just off Lumley Road. They stashed their Parkas in the luggage lockers of the bikes (why spend a fortune on clothes only to conceal them from view with army surplus?). Milt tilted his head to the sky, his sun glasses were coated in a film of road dust. 'Like the lady says,' he said, sniffing the air 'the weekend starts here.'

'Yeah - sea breezes, windy beaches, moving dunes.' Skegness always brought Andy's submerged romantic streak to the surface.

'Fish and chips, Worthington E, and fanny - that's where it's at.' Don, the realist, confirmed. 'So don't forget what you're about Andy - right!'

Andy said nothing, but stretched his arms high above his head in an attempt to remove the aches of the journey. So maybe it wasn't "Surf City", but it was good enough. The weekend stretched out before them - as eventful as they wanted to make it.
'I'm starving, ' Don said, 'let's go to "The Brief".'
'I need some pills.' Milt added. 'If I can remember this weekend on Tuesday it'll have been a drag!' Lord knows, he thought, he had enough in his head to forget. They trooped across to the café. The door was open and as they approached they heard the fruits of someone's Jukebox selection - Len Barry's "1-2-3". It was so easy? The place was teeming with Mods. They exchanged greetings with some of the people they were already acquainted with and eyed and evaluated those who were strangers to them. There were Parkas everywhere; some draped over the back of chairs, others piled on the floor.

Whilst eating in silence they soaked up the ambience of a generation in flux, driven by the changing whims of fashion, music and manner. It was a style which came straight from the street. Andy marvelled at the inventiveness of it all - coloured cotton T shirts displayed beneath three buttoned, basket woven sports shirts, faded demin, which looked as if it had been shrink wrapped on the limbs it covered. A youth from Stamford had customised an old school blazer, replacing the badge from the breast pocket with an embroidered emblem of an RAF Fighter Squadron, wings and all. (Op art - you saw it first in Lincolnshire.) The youth had left the maroon braiding on every edge of the blue serge jacket, cheap but stunningly effective, when worn with a pair of maroon hipsters and blue Hush Puppie shoes. Another lad, an apprentice butcher, sported his blue and white cotton butcher's jacket - scrubbed clean of its usual coating of pig's blood, it could easily have come from the window of a Carnaby Street boutique.

There were girls with tight fitting, ribbed sweaters, with deep welted cuffs and bottoms - plain, striped and some in up-to-the-minute square blocks of colour, fashioned in white, black and bright, paint box colours, polo necked, scooped or crew, loose fitting sports shirts, short and long sleeved, teamed with trousers, jeans or skirts of varying lengths. The mini skirt had, by this time, lost favour with the Mod girls and skirt lengths were now touching or well below the knee.

The girls' hair styles varied from the short Mod crop to the long, straight locks of the Marianne Faithfull/Francoise Hardy chanteuse genre. Andy preferred the short style on a girl, Milt's preference veered towards the shoulder length and beyond - Don couldn't care a monkey's as long as she was a looker and went in and out at all the right places.

The girls' choice of footwear was (almost) always soft Hush Puppies, tied with double knots, although Andy had been talking to some girls from Peterborough who were, they'd told him, "going posh", in wearing slightly higher heeled T bars and sling backs, with a more traditional, tailored look to their fabrics. He looked around at the avant garde spectacular enacted before his eyes. "The Posh" from Peterborough hadn't arrived - yet.

In a corner, two youths, with hair pulled forward in mock Beatles style, were in grey double breasted reefer jackets; both looked like refugees from another world. Out of touch and out of time, they were either ignored or ridiculed by the Mods in the café. They were as outdated as the messages with telephone numbers scrawled on the café's walls in previous weeks. A month was a long time in the 60s.

Outside in the street a group of Mods from Leicester filed past the door of the café, chanting something which Andy couldn't make out - apart from two words - "Grease" and "Bastards". They were (boys and girls) mainly dressed in greys and blues. The bulk of the group wore long petrol blue nylon rain macs - poor man's leathers. Andy smiled inwardly, he knew all about that.

The three of them finished their meal and Milt took his jacket off, complaining of the heat. He was wearing what Andy recognised as a Newark Castle Cycling Club racing vest. The Tricel body of the shirt was royal blue and the elasticated sleeves and neck were bright yellow.

Worn with Milt's newly bleached jeans, against a deep tan from the sun and wind of an almost rainless summer, the vest looked perfect.
'Where'd you get the fabric Maverick?' Andy asked Milt, fingering the slippery material.
'My cousin was binning it,' Milt said casually, ' 'thought it might come in useful.' Too true, Andy thought.
' 'looks good.' Andy said wistfully. 'Ain't he riding anymore?'
'No, the prat's getting married - selling all his bikes and gear. I mean fancy having to sell your push bike to get shacked up with somebody - I wouldn't sell my GS for anybody.'
'How much d' you give for the shirt?' Andy asked.
'Sod all - I told you he was ditching it. How much d'you part with for yours?' Milt said, picking at the end of one of the black vinyl stripes.
'Thirty bob.' Andy said.
'You were robbed!' Don chimed in, laughing.

Andy felt he had been.

The selector arm of the Jukebox moved silently and mysteriously along its track, stooped forward and with its magic steel claw, pulled another vinyl circle from the long black waiting row. Its return journey to the turntable was tantalisingly brief. The chords of "My Generation" were sucked in and spat out of the speakers above their heads. The song blitzed the café and the immediate vicinity of the street. The trio sipped the last of their tea and followed the song outside.

They began to walk down to the Clock Tower on the sea front. Their promenade was curtailed by a khaki clad Mod on a scooter, who braked his bike to a standstill in their paths.
'Hiya Lincoln.' Don said, smiling. 'Didn't see you on the road.'
'One of our mob had some trouble back at Horncastle - took us an hour to get the carb cleaned out.' the Mod confirmed.
'What's the crack then Laz?' Milt asked the youth.
'Dunno really.' Laz said, still astride his scooter, 'I heard there's a load of Lincoln grease gonna blow in on Sunday.
'Save'em for Milt.' Andy joined the discourse.
'Hey!' said Laz, almost as an after thought, 'I've heard the Posh Boys are in town with "The Smiler".'

' 'that right?' Don said, bristling.
'Yeah,' Laz went on, 'I've heard they've got a caravan crammed full of gear somewhere out at Ingoldmells - Butlins' way.'
'Sounds like the same stunt they were pulling at Yarmouth a couple of weeks back.' Andy said.
'Ten to one my back rack's on special offer.' said Milt drily.
' 'fancy a ride out there Laz?' Don asked.
'No, I'll see you later on - I'd better find our crowd - before they get into trouble!' He laughed and kick started his scooter.
'Where're you kippin' tonight?' Milt enquired of the Lincoln youth.
'Down on the beach probably.' Laz replied. 'Pop, Harry and the rest of the Sutton scooter lads'll be there, near the old amphibian. Should be some decent shelter.'
'I'd sooner sleep out in the open, under the stars, like we used to in Scouts.' Andy said wistfully.
'Prat!' Milt said tersely, looking at Andy.
Laz rode off down the sea front to a chorus of 'See you laters'.

*

'If we don't find it soon we're back to the town.' Don said angrily, halting his scooter at the umpteenth Ingoldmells caravan site they had scoured, looking for the Peterborough Mods. Milt rode aimlessly in a tight circle in the entrance to the site. Andy raised himself by standing full height on the running board of Don's bike, shielding his eyes from the sun, as he surveyed the area.
'I can see the roofs of some vans behind the trees over there.' he said pointing to an entrance in a tree lined field, whose sign was partly obscured by the summer foliage.
'One last shot.' Don said, moving off in the direction Andy had suggested. Milt followed.

The field was a large one, full of caravans, some occupied, some for sale or rent. The two scooters moved slowly and methodically down the lines of caravans, laid out in a neat grid pattern; each van equidistant from the next.

'Still nothing.' Milt said, drawing alongside Don and Andy.
'Got it!' said Andy from the pillion. 'Scooters over there.'
Don and Milt turned their bikes to the right towards a large static caravan at the end of a row. There were five scooters, chromed up to the gunnels, parked, side by side, in front of a white caravan. The words - "The Posh" - in red letters on one of the bikes' fly screens, depicted the origins of the Vespas and Lambrettas. Two green mini-vans were parked nearby. In the centre doorway of the caravan a tall Mod youth stood, looking down condescendingly from the top of the steps.

' 'giving Green Shields?' Milt said, as he pushed his way past the sentry at the door.
'Newark - the original jokers.' said the Mod as he followed Milt into the caravan. He hovered like a Burton's shop assistant. Don and Andy followed in pursuit of their friend.

There were six other Peterborough Mods inside and the caravan was racked out with a long row of leather and suede coats of varying lengths, styles and colours, assembled for general sale. The stock of garments was the fruits of numerous cloakroom scams, worked on clubs from Sheffield to Stevenage and occasional clandestine forays into C & A's on crowded Saturday afternoons.

The two wheeled contingent was also catered for, with a dazzling display of two-stroke chrome work, stacked neatly at the back of the van. Front and back racks, mirrors, spot lamps, pennants, flags, spare wheels and chrome side panels were on sale - no reasonable offer refused. Milt, Andy and Don looked around the Aladdin's cave. Andy fingered some of the suede coats as he walked along the rail. There was an uneasy atmosphere, fuelled by mutual dislike and distrust between camps. The three Newark Mods had no time for those individuals who rode motorbikes - they generated a feeling of disgust - but there was an odd sort of tempered respect for the grease, which may have only existed in their collective sub-consciousness. There was however little affinity with this particular band of Mods, of the same tribal persuasions, who plundered the possessions of factions of their own clan.

' 'you buying or just looking?' said another of the custodians.
' 'depends what the gear is.' Don replied coolly.

'We don't want any of this shit!' Milt said tersely. 'It's all rolled - thieving bastards!'
'All top quality merchandise Newark - something for everybody.'
'And everything's somebody's.' Andy said. At Andy's remark a youth arose from the window seat of the caravan. This was "The Smiler". He was the top Mod from Peterborough - hard as nails. ***The*** *Face.*

' 'you dealing in gear?' Milt said, moving over to the two wheeled paraphernalia.
'Could be.....then perhaps we couldn't be.'

Milt ignored the last two comments as he picked out a Vespa's chrome back rack from the stack of equipment and started to scrutinise it.
'The gear we've got doesn't bear talking about Newark - heavy, heavy, heavy.' "The Smiler" grinned. At this moment Milt lunged towards him, brandishing the rear rack. 'You thieving bastard!' Milt shouted. 'This is my rack!'

Instantly, a quartet of the Posh Boys closed ranks, one of them grabbing the chrome work from Milt's hand. All four of them formed a faded denim and cotton clad shield in front of "The Smiler". The others stood behind the Newark youths.
' 'not your rack at all Newark.' "The Smiler" spoke from behind the press of bodies. 'Three notes and it could be though.'

Milt was pushing against the Peterborough Mods. The two camps were standing off each other. Don was cool. Andy was petrified.
'You lousy robbing ....'
'Leave it Milt - save it.' Don interrupted him, his hand on Milt's shoulder, pulling him away, slowly.

The Newark youths backed out of the caravan. Don turned to the Mods still inside. 'You're living on borrowed time.' Don said coldly.
'The Nottingham crowd's coming down to see to you.' Milt spat his words.
"Oh see how we quake in our Hush Puppies.' came a voice from the doorway.

Don and Andy mounted the Lambretta and started to move away from the caravan. Andy looked round to see Milt and his scooter disappearing in the opposite direction up the field. Andy's puzzled look soon dissolved, as Milt turned his bike around and sped back towards the caravan.

'Ride!' Andy urged, as he saw Milt's left foot, held out sideways at right angles, like a chariot's scimitar, smash into the front rack of the first scooter parked outside the caravan. The bike toppled off its stand and brought the other four scooters down with it, like a set of collapsing dominos.

The three of them reached Skegness town before catching their breath outside "The Jolly Fisherman", on the front.

'We should have had a go at 'em. That was definitely my rack.' Milt complained.

'Oh yeah,' Don replied, 'seven plays three - I've always wanted to be declared a national disaster area.'

*

There were a few minor skirmishes between black leather and khaki during the rest of the afternoon, but the hordes of Lincoln Grease, which Laz had said were to form part of the weekend's proceedings, had so far failed to materialise. They had cruised around the town with the other Mods, soaking up the sunshine and contributing to the general traffic chaos of any English seaside town, filling up for a Bank Holiday weekend. Forget Rome, Andy thought - today, all roads led to Skegness.

Back in "The Brief Encounter" they had tapped into the grapevine which kept this culture alive and vibrant. Chatting with Mods from the hinterland, they had heard of a youth from Leicester, who had been fined £10 on the spot by the Lincolnshire police for speeding and of another, from London, who had been in court when the acres of chrome on his bike had dazzled a motorist, sending him spinning off into a ditch one sunny afternoon earlier in the Summer.

Of such notoriety are priceless reputations born.

So far, Milt had been unable to locate his private supply of pep pills and had been begging, buying or borrowing enough Amphetamine on a piecemeal basis, which was so far proving just sufficient for his desired state of drug induced forgetfulness. Pills were being popped freely in the cafés and parks and in the streets. French Blues, Bombers, Purple Hearts were being consumed by the handful.

Why wait? Live now, pay later - that perfect leitmotif for the 60s would eventually extract its chemical and biological revenge as the kids would, at some time during the weekend, have to come down from the cliffs they were presently scaling.

In this precious part of the county roads were blocked with traffic - and Mods were blocked with pills.

The three of them rapped on a variety of heartfelt topics. On fashion - leather v. suede. Side vents v. centre vents. Stripes v. squares. On music - Tamla Motown v. Soul. Small Faces v. The Who. Georgie Fame v. Long John Baldry. Brothers Righteous v. Brothers Walker. Otis Redding v. James Brown.

On how even Dylan was turning on to the kinetics of the culture, swopping the Triumph motorcycle T shirt on the cover of "Highway 61 Revisited" to the tab collared Mod from the gatefold sleeve of "Blonde on Blonde". They discussed two-stroke modes of transport. Lambretta v. Vespa. (Innocenti v. Piaggio.) LI v. GS. They argued about clubs - Mojo, Sheffield v. Dungeon, Nottingham. Black Cat, Huddersfield v. The Face, Grantham. Twisted Wheel, Manchester v. Marquee, London. Peephole, Leicester v. Clouds, Derby.

They had ridden out to the south of the town, to witness the spectacle of Mods (from Peterborough to Preston) racing their bikes against each other, and the clock, using the road out to Gibraltar Point as a makeshift drag strip. The fastest had been a Mod from Stamford, called John Leddington, whose new Lambretta GT200 had blown away all its opposition. Andy had drooled over the sleek lines of the bike and its £200 plus price tag.

They had bought pennants, as souvenirs of the weekend, from local shops, whose sense of wariness and animosity towards this itinerant army of intruders was slaked only by the increase in revenue brought with it. Throughout the slow, mannered build up towards Saturday night in Skegness the Mods accepted and revelled in their status as Lincolnshire's least desirable.

*

Anybody who was anybody had packed themselves into the "Bass House" pub on the northern end of the Prom, where the management, eager to tap into the Saturday night spending power of the Mods, had done their homework in booking a local R 'n' B group, backed up by a disco. The DJ's playlist of records was perfect for the kids - barely accessible Tamla material - early Supremes, Martha Reeves and the Vandellas - he played a perfect mixture, including Charlie and Inez Foxx, Sam and Dave, Booker T and the MG's, Beach Boys, Who and Them.

And not a Cliff Richard record within earshot.

While the group were on stage, pumping out their tightly performed versions of classic rhythm and blues songs - "Dimples", "Got My Mojo Working", "Smokestack Lightning", "Hoochie Coochie man" et al - the Mods, in the main, gathered around the stage listening to and watching the group, who, on occasions, turned their backs on the audience to concentrate on their instrumental exchanges and interactions. The group was a five piece set up, featuring traditional line up and instrumentation, with emphasis on guitar in the form of bass, rhythm and lead, backed by a drummer and fronted by a lead singer, who also played harmonica.

The pub, thus transformed into makeshift dance hall, was noisy, hot, smelly, sweaty and overcrowded. Andy loved every minute of it. Earlier in the evening after the start of the group's first session, Milt had latched on to a blonde haired girl from Sleaford and had spent the best part of the night in a corner, trying to get his point of view into her head and his hands under her sweater. With Milt thus engaged, Don and Andy were transformed into a far more efficient pulling machine.

The disco was a couple of records old when Don stuck his mouth into Andy's ear.

' 'don't like yours Andy.' Don shouted and pointed to a couple of girls dancing around their handbags in the middle of the floor and, as yet, unattached.

'Piss off!' Andy said. 'You stitched me up at Leicester last week!' Andy complained. They had an agreement that, when picking up girls, they each took it in turns to choose the better looking of a pair - such was a Mod boy's skin depth approach to both fashion and the female sex. In

the main this worked well as their tastes, though similar, were not identical. On the last few occasions however, Don had worked him over and Andy was still smarting from the results of some of the strokes Don had pulled and the effect it was having on his reputation among his peers, who judged you on the quality of the clothes you wore and the company you kept.

*On this occasion however Don had joked, for there was nothing to choose between the two girls, who had already been giving Don and Andy the vibes, in the form of eye contact and heavily suggestive body language in the form of their dancing. Don and Andy moved across the floor towards the girls and Don, ever practical, chose the nearest. The connection was made and the four danced together, around the girls' handbags for the next few songs. The music was so loud that meaningful conversation was impossible until each record had finished. From the few words, which did pass between Andy and the girl between songs, it was apparent that there was a mutual attraction. Before long, Don escorted his dancing companion from the floor, in the direction of the bar. Andy asked his partner if she wanted to join Don, but she refused, wishing to stay on the dance floor. This fitted in perfectly with what was in Andy's head, but more importantly, with what money **wasn't** in his pocket. The purchase of his suit and sports shirt had, as usual, almost skinted him; but dancing, like laughter, is a great leveller and out there on the floor, swaying in time with someone who shared his passion for music and dancing, he was anyone's equal (with or without money).*

The girl was, Andy thought, an incredible dancer. She had that visceral connection with, and affinity to, the pulse and thrust of the songs the DJ was filling their heads with. They danced non-stop for what seemed like hours. They moved provocatively towards and away from each other, in what had become a precious collection of private moments in front of a public address system. They turned their backs on each other, occasionally seeking eye contact, alternatively refusing it. She interpreted each song in a different manner, capturing its mood and nuance. Andy found inspiration from the girl's movements and matched her, step for step. He was sweating from the exertion but refused to take off the jacket to his suit. The weight of the cloth felt reassuringly heavy, as it swirled around his hips and slid across his chest. He had, nor desired, the words to describe how completely natural it felt, dancing in his street clothes. If asked, he would have acknowledged that the feeling lay rooted more in Cathy McGowan and "Ready Steady Go!" than in "Come Dancing".

If Milt, on occasions, would get out of his brain with pills, in his attempt to achieve a state of temporary amnesia, dancing, for Andy, was his way of obliterating the realities and pressures which underpinned his life as a Mod in the 60s. The factory where he was completing the first stages of a technical apprenticeship was thus evicted from his head, blotting out the rattle of machinery and the narrow-minded attitude of the engineering industry.

Dancing, for Andy, was a serious business.

As the evening drew to its close, the end of the disco was heralded by the DJ's customary announcement over the PA system and his revised choice of records. The soft tempos induced a state of smoochiness in those left on the floor. The sense of panic and frustration, portrayed on the faces of boys and girls who hadn't pulled, increased in direct proportion to the reduction in available dancing time. There was a sudden influx of people onto the floor as the lights were dimmed to complement the mood created by the music. The first few chords of The Moody Blues" song crept seductively from the speakers and seemed to hang above the dance floor in its smoky stratosphere. Andy and the girl moved together, instinctively and with arms and legs locking, swayed gently in a private cocoon at the centre of the crush and swell.

"We've already said .... goodbye"

Her hips pressed into his groin and his trousers changed shape.

"I don't want you to tell me just what you to intend to do now....

He responded by sliding his hands under her sweater. It fitted where it touched, which was everywhere. His fingers glided along the warm film of sweat trickling down her back guiding him to the seams of her bra straps. He squeezed her breasts, feeling the hardness of her nipples pressing tightly underneath the fabric.

but how many times do I have to tell you.......

She responded by placing her tongue in his mouth and her right hand inside his trousers. She grasped. He gasped.

darling, darling, I'm still in love, still in love ..."

The soft slow meandering of their fingertips was layered up with husky voiced vocal against heavy orchestral backing.

And thus they hung on to the song, marvelling at the musical world of unseen touch and tease beneath their clothes.

The song faded and as the other dancers waited for its replacement, the girl took hold of Andy's hand and led him in the direction of the exit. They pushed their way through the Mods and into the street. The night was warm, still. August. The street was awash with the chrome of what must have been a hundred and fifty scooters.

Nearby, a small group of Mods were animated and shouting. They had formed a circle around a youth, well out of his head on a chemical diet of Blues and burgers, who held the black leather jacket of a greaser between his finger tips - keeping it at arm's length, as if it was diseased. The youth shook it towards each of the Mods, who shrank from the silver studded garment, shrieking and giggling hysterically. The group virtually cracked up with laughter as the Mod boy holding the jacket let it drop to the floor and proceeded to urinate over it.

Andy turned and looked back to "The Bass House" pub, still full of Mods and music. For some strange reason (or not so strange) his subconscious dredged up a poem from his school days. It raged in his head -

Do you remember an Inn,
Miranda?
Do you remember an Inn?
And the tedding and the spreading
Of the straw for a bedding,

And the cheers and the jeers of the young muleteers
Who hadn't got a penny,
And who weren't paying any
And the hammer at the doors and the Din?
And the Hip! Hop! Hap!

Of the clap
Of the hands to the twirl and the swirl
Of the girl gone chancing,
Glancing,
Dancing,

Hilaire Belloc (1870-1953)

"Tarantella" - drummed into his head so many times in his English classes. What a bummer, Andy thought - having to die before the 60s.

The weekend was fitting together so perfectly - Andy was reminded of that perfection, feeling the pull of the girl on his arm as she moved across the road, towards the dunes. The sounds of the sea competed with music and conversation.

*

"What's the time?'
'Dunno - about half one.' Milt replied to Don's question.
The pair of them were parked up near the pier, lounging on the seats of their bikes.
'Who'd Andy end up with?' Milt asked.
'Someone from Louth - I saw him sloping off towards the beach with her.' Don replied. There was a tone of satisfaction in his voice.
'How d'you go?' Milt asked.
Don smiled and turned to Milt.
'You know what they say about red heads.'
'She wasn't a red head.' Milt said looking puzzled.
'No - but her old man was - and could he run!' Milt smiled. 'What about you?' Don asked.
'Waste of time,' Milt confessed, 'first she said she would - but then she wouldn't.

The pair mulled over the dramas, comedies and tragedies of the weekend so far. The sound of the occasional two-stroke engine could be heard in the streets of the sleepy town behind them. Dickie Valentine smiled benignly down on them.

'Where're we kipping?' Milt asked.

'Laz says everybody's going down the dunes - 'you game?'

'Nah.' Milt said. 'Don't fancy sand in my goolies. Perhaps Peterborough'll lend us their caravan.' he added drily.

'Hey, do you remember those two we met at "The Mojo" the other week - they came from the Skeg area.' Don sparked.

'Yeah - Pigsville.' Milt said.

'Hogsthorpe - you prat! 's just down the road - they said we could look 'em up this weekend.'

' 'you get a promise then?' Milt shot Don a sly look.

'Their parents are away for a couple of weeks.' Don added, with a gleam in his eye and got up from the Lambretta's seat. He turned on the petrol tap of the scooter and kicked the bike over, but it failed to start. He cursed. Milt remained draped across the GS's seat.

'Well what're you hanging about for?' Don turned to Milt and switched the petrol off to prevent the cylinders from flooding.

'Donny boy, we aint got their address.' Milt said emphatically. 'It's on the wall in "The Brief" - but it's two in the morning and "The Brief's" closed, right!'

'You wrote it down, didn't you?' Don quizzed him.

'Yeah - on a Rizla paper.' Milt remained in reclining mode.

'Well?'

' 'smoked it didn't I.' he turned and smiled broadly in Don's direction.

'Milt - you're a waste of space!'

'Donald - flattery will get you everywhere.'

Their conversation was halted by the sound of half a dozen scooters, the staccato popping of the two-strokes was followed shortly by the arrival of Laz and his crowd from Lincoln. There were girls on all but two of the pillions. The youths who carried the ladies were those who revved their engines the loudest.

'Hiya Lincoln.' Don and Milt acknowledged the clan - most of them were as high as a Proby top note.
'We've heard somebody's throwing a party down Drummond Road.' The owner of the voice washed his words down with a couple of pills.
'Yeah,' you coming Newark?' Laz urged.
'We're coming.' Milt said, buttoning up his Parka.
'Where's Andy?' one of the girls asked.
'Last time we saw him he was disappearing into the dunes with a lover from Louth.' Don said and started his bike up.

A police car cruised slowly by and they all exchanged uneasy glances with its occupants. Both mouths and throttles were shut and conversation ceased until the car had passed.
'I saw Andy with her at the gig.' the girl on Laz's pillion said, 'Two tugs and she's anybody's.'
'Slag!' another girl confirmed.
'Hey Milt,' said a voice from the back, 'we saw your raver from Sheffield.'

Milt grimaced.
"She was asking about you - 'did you a favour. We told her you'd started at Butlins!' The Lincoln crowd laughed. Even Milt saw the funny side of this - the girl's obsessive crush, in which he was the chief object of desire.
' 'bet she spent the night playing Bingo, waiting for the end of your shift.' the youth added.

By this time Milt was astride his bike, engine throbbing.
'Do you wanna go find Andy?' Laz said to Don.
'No - leave him - a night out on his own'll do him good!' Don smiled.
The group moved off along the prom in the direction of Drummond Road.

Meanwhile, on another part of the coast, Don's issued command was Andy's earnest wish. He was losing his virginity.

Of the hands to the twirl and the swirl
Of the girl gone chancing,
Glancing,
Dancing,
Backing and advancing,
Snapping of the clapper to the spin
Out and in -

*

There were about thirty scooters outside the house which stood at the end of what, before this weekend, was a quiet cul-de-sac. The music was loud and the lights of most of the houses in the road were lit; nobody in the neighbourhood was to get much sleep in the foreseeable future. Don, Milt, Laz and the rest of the Lincoln crowd parked up and added themselves to the crush of bodies in the house.

The Dansette record player was turned up to full volume and the front speaker vibrated with the strength of the bass note on each of the records. A pile of black vinyl was stacked on the machine's autochanger - they clattered, one by one, down the central spindle onto the turntable, hurtling round at 45 rpm.

The Garrard stylus picked up every crackle and scratch in the well worn grooves and belched them, with the song, out into the room. Some of the Mods were dancing on the make-shift dance floor, with all the furniture having been removed to the garage or pushed up against the walls.

The party goers, most of whose material worth could be measured by the clothes they possessed, had scant regard for the property of others and the fabric of the house and the studious care which had been invested in it, was now being slowly, but radically, rearranged. The carpet already had several burn holes (Woodbines and Hush Puppies) and some particularly evil looking stains had appeared thereon (Party Sevens and swizzle stick stomachs). The wallpaper in the kitchen was splattered with liquid, (cider and unsteady hands),three panes were broken in the glass door between the kitchen and the hall (two boys and only one girl).

'Fine party.' Milt said and smiled at Don as they made their way into the front room, pushing themselves past the dancers in the middle of the floor. Two girls sorting records for the next refill of the Dansette were descended upon by Don and Milt and within a couple of minutes all four of them were dancing to the Tamla on the turntable.

Adrenalin and Amphetamine kept the party travelling on towards its rendezvous with the dawn.

'Turn the light off!' The shout was answered by a Mackeson bottle smashing into the lampshade - glass showered on the floor - the naked filament of the bulb hung live yet useless in the bayonet socket.

The newly created dusk of the room and the reduction in the music's tempo, curtesy of the newly stacked auto-changer, altered the body language of the dancers..... tongues sought mouths, fingers loosened buttons, zips and fastenings; arms and legs intertwined and whisperings in ears became more provocative and suggestive. The dance floor cleared - couples wandered off outside or up the stairs. Milt eventually led his partner from the floor, making their way through the hall and up the stairs, past the bodies of the revellers, some leaning against the walls talking, kissing, cajoling - some sitting on the floor and several lying on the landing, presently taking no active part in the proceedings. They made their way to the back bedroom - the bed was occupied by two couples in the throes of having sex, in varying stages of undress, cavorting on top of the pile of coats and Parkas. Another boy and girl were grappling on a rug beside the sleeping figure of a youth from Peterborough, one of the group whose bikes had been floored by Milt on the previous afternoon.

The next bedroom offered them no better place to lay themselves down and they moved to the large front bedroom. The bed there was occupied by one of the Lincoln Mods and the girl who had been his pillion passenger - they were top to tail with Don and the girlfriend of Milt's present partner. Typical, Milt thought, looking around the room. Along one wall was a huge Victorian wardrobe - a press. Milt led the girl past another couple on the floor and opened up one of the large doors. He pushed the clothes to the far end of the rail which ran the whole length of the unit and looked inside, he turned, smiled at the girl and bolstered up the floor with a covering of blankets, which had been stacked neatly on the end section of horizontal shelves.

The pair of them stepped inside and closed the doors behind them.

*

The parents of the girl who had thrown the party returned home earlier than they had planned. They had been contacted by neighbours and their weekend had finished in the early hours of Sunday morning.

They arrived back to find that the majority of the party crowd had departed - only a solitary Vespa GS was still parked in the road. They came home to find the flower beds in the front and back gardens flattened and the lawns they had cut and rolled for years criss-crossed with deep furrows, scarred by the wheels of the scooters, which had been ridden across them.

They found the interior in no better condition. The banister rail was broken in several places, carpets were piebald with beer stains and cigarette burns. There were several window panes broken - the glass lay on the patio and on the paths around the house.

The girl was crying and her mother, all colour drained from her face, was in a state of shock. The man was walking around the house shaking his head in disbelief. He slowly climbed the stairs and looked in at the state of the bedrooms. Entering the main bedroom he turned to the creaking of the wardrobe door and watched, incredulously, as Milt emerged from the wardrobe, shielding his eyes from the early morning light.

'Fine party.' Milt said and stumbled past the man, who looked on in disbelief, rooted to the spot, as Milt made his way gingerly down the stairs and out to the road, leaving his cohabitee still asleep in the wardrobe.

***

UNDER THE BOARD WALK

Andy found Don lying on a bench in the gardens close to the Boating Lake. Milt was underneath it. They were both covered with their Parkas. The two scooters were parked up nearby. All three sleeping bags were still rolled up neatly and fastened to the racks of the scooters. They hadn't been touched since they were strapped there on the Saturday afternoon. It was now about 7 o'clock on the Sunday morning. The morning after the disco. The morning after the party after the disco - and for Andy **the** *morning after.*

Both Don and Milt were asleep. Andy, on the other hand, was well awake. He had sauntered up to them with a spring in his step and the air of someone who had lost half a crown but just found a ten bob note. He carried his Parka over his shoulder, awash with a new nonchalance. The morning was again blue, fresh and vibrant - in marked contrast to the state of his friends - haggard, horizontal, and for the moment, inert.

He sat down on a bench opposite and leaned back over the top rail, offering his face to the sun, which was starting its morning climb over the North Sea. He closed his eyes and let the rays soak into and through him. One of the back stripes of insulation tape on his sports shirt was hanging loose by a few inches - a poignant reminder to him of the events of the night. He opened his eyes and a series of floaters, created by the sun within his eyes, drifted down to earth before him like a monochromatic light show and its collection of magnified, microscopic images.

The town was just starting to awake and steel itself for the hurly burly of another day in high summer season. A couple walking their dog, passed between him and his sleeping friends. He smiled, but the homely gesture was not returned. Their dog, a mongrel of terrier extract, sniffed along the length of Milt's prone form, cocked its leg against the wrought iron side of the bench and then left in pursuit of its master. The warm puddle of liquid trickled slowly down the slight incline towards Milt. Andy watched in silent mirth at the progress of this liquid alarm clock. It seeped beneath Milt's Parka and Milt awoke abruptly, cursing, rolling away from the stream of dog pee. In the course of Milt's evasive action he banged his head on the underside of the bench, thereby waking Don from his slumber on the top level of their makeshift bunk.

What Milt was going to do to the dog was RSPCA classified. Don and Milt were thus introduced to another glorious day on the Lincolnshire Riviera.

'You two look like death.' Andy greeted them, as they finally came to terms with the morning.

'Then just let me die then.' Milt moaned.

Don was about to go back to sleep when Andy got up and walked across to him. He took the hood of Don's Parka.

'C'mon. You need some fresh air.' Andy urged.

'Andy - piss off!' Don snapped.

'I need a fresh head.' Milt complained.

'Come on.' Andy addressed the pair of them. 'Let's go out to the creek. The tide'll be in and the wind'll be fresh up.'

Don was motionless.

'C'mon Don!' Andy was insistent. 'You can go on the back.'

Robotically, Don seated himself astride his scooter and slumped against the back rest. Andy walked over to Milt's scooter and started it up. 'Now all you've gotta do is point it Milt - follow me.' Andy said, walking back to the Lambretta, which he also kicked into life. Don, still half asleep, was jolted upright by the thud of the LI's stand against the running boards underneath his feet. As Andy selected first gear and twisted the throttle Don tapped Andy lightly on the shoulder. Andy turned around as Don spoke. 'D'you make it last night then?'

'Yeah.....'

As he was about to expand, extol, amplify and embroider his journey of a lifetime,he noticed Don had fallen asleep.

They moved off down through the gardens past the sign which read "No Motor Vehicles Beyond This Point" and onto the road.

Milt followed - somehow.

A short ride later found them negotiating a narrow shale track, just north of the town. It led down through the dunes to the beach. With a fresh on-shore breeze and high tide, the sunlight on the water transformed it into a shimmering mantle of liquid quicksilver. Andy walked down across the dunes for a couple of paces. Although he didn't notice it, the green of the Maram grasses, which bound the dunes together and moved at the whim of the wind, was the exact colour of his suit.

Andy's seminal experiences in the hours after the disco had been typical - wrought from Saturday night sexuality - wet, wild, fumbling, impatient, but incredibly exciting. Already he was romanticising about it. He started to hum a recent Donovan song, as the wind blew his hair to and fro.

The soft, lilting tune of "Catch The Wind", floating on the ebb and flow of the tide, was the perfect music for the mood he had created for himself.

He'd locked the image of himself and the girl deep inside his head, purified, glorified - an icon. If the girls from Lincoln were to be believed she was, at this moment, probably in a caravan down the road, relieving another adolescent of the burden of his underwear.

He stood, looking out over the ocean, shielding his eyes with the palms of his hands. He had never seen the sea look so mysterious, so ethereal, but then in the last frenetic year or so he'd never taken the time out to look. All the vital moments and memories of his life were seemingly distilled into this one wordless time and place. He sat down at the top of the dunes and gazed on, mesmerised.

'Incredible.' he whistled through his teeth.

Don snored. Milt puked.

*

The couple of hours they'd spent out at the dunes in the freshening wind and the ride back into Skegness town completed the awakening process of both Don and Milt (Andy was already as high as the kites now flapping above the north beach). By the time they were cruising past the pier, on the front, all three had smiles to rival the shiny white teeth of Dickie Valentine on the left and the zest for life, depicted by the brightly painted figure in "The Jolly Fisherman" pub sign, on the right.

Their first stop before breakfast at "The Brief Encounter" was at the toilets and wash room at the top of the road where the café stood. As they rounded the traffic island, which contained the clock tower amidst its carpet of summer flowers, they saw the rows of scooters, parked up at right angles to the pavement. The owners of the bikes were already in the throes of their communal ablutions in the wash room as the three of them descended the stairs into the toilets.

The room was full of Mods, most of them bare to the waist, in the middle of strip washes. Parkas and T shirts were draped over improvised hangers - door handles, tops of doors and dog bolts. Funny, Andy thought as he looked around, how everyone looks the same without their street clothes. Some of the Mods were in the process of shaving in front of the long mirror, which spanned the whole of the side wall above the wash-basins, they turned at Don, Milt and Andy's entrance and muttered various garbled greetings from beneath white beards of shaving foam.

The three of them found a wash-basin to share, which had just been vacated by one of their acquaintances from Lincoln; as Don and Milt started to strip off their T shirts Andy busied himself by flushing away some strange and disgusting looking substance, which lay congealing in the bottom of the bowl. He winced at the sight, looked round and saw the back of the youth, who was responsible for the deposit in the basin, treading gingerly on each of the steps - one hand on the banister rail, the other clutching his stomach, as he climbed up to the street.

The last vestige of what had filled the bowl was disappearing down the plug hole by the time Don and Milt were ready to start their ablutions. Typical, Andy thought, he'd found another of his true vocations - Don and Milt's private janitor. Andy stood back and let Don and Milt share the single wash-basin in the room, already full.

He watched combs and hair brushes, working in determined (and sometimes desperate) attempts to restore and repair the ravages of whatever sleeping arrangements had been made by the Mods during the Saturday night before - the beach, benches, boats from the lake and the bandstand had provided makeshift beds for hordes of unpaying and unwanted guests of the town. Other Mods were paying meticulous attention to every last detail of their appearance; for this was another day - another dress-up.

Andy noticed how such a disproportionate amount of time was spent by the boys in getting their hair just right before they went out into the light and waiting onlookers. He recalled how a year and a half ago it had taken at least two months of experimenting, of trial and error, of cutting and shaping, to transform his forward swept Beatle cut into the classic Mod crop it was now. Most of the Mods, including Andy, either cut their hair themselves or let their friends do it. None of them were prepared to let the "short back and sides" obsession of some scissor happy barber ruin, in a couple of minutes, what had taken months to create.

(In the early days as a Mod he had merely combed the hair straight back from his forehead and then pulled the sides down, creating some semblance of a centre parting but had only managed to keep this in place for a few minutes until the wind in the street had scallywagged it back into floppy Beatle cut. Eventually he had cropped it shorter on the top and feather cut it down the sides and back. This shorter version created just the right amount of height over the crown, in true Mod cropped style. He'd stood for hours before the mirror above the mantle piece in his back room, armed with hand mirror, viewing the results of his coiffure from every angle.) Surveying the efforts of the kids in front of the mirror he was, in terms of hairstyle, exactly where he needed to be.

He started to daydream as Don and Milt splashed around the basin before him and recalled the look of some of the Mod bands he'd seen in recent times - he marvelled at the shape and colour of Daltrey's hair and the soft, but stylish, locks of Stevie Marriott: but the most outrageous and exaggerated style of Mod crop had been sported by a guy whom he'd seen in the Nottingham "Dungeon" Club, at the back end of last year, performing a short set of four or five songs, sandwiched between the two sessions of Long John Baldry's band. In "The Royal Children" pub on Castle Gate, into which "The Dungeon" crowd spilled after the group's stint, Andy and his friends had been talking to this singer, who spoke and sang like he had a mouth full of razor blades. Andy had been fascinated by his hair cut, swearing it was back combed up on his crown. He could see the man now, in blue crew necked sweater, downing pints of bitter in the pub, holding court among the Mods - Rod Stewart - Hoochie Coochie Man.

His thoughts tracked back to the days of his first fashion fads (and a burgeoning awareness of the power of clothes) when, in early '63, he could have been seen hobbling down his street in two inch Cuban heeled boots, decked out in a brown elephant cord Beatle jacket with its rounded mandarin collar. What a prat, he now thought he must have looked, in those first stages of metamorphosis from Beatle Boy look-alike to fully fledged Mod.

He lived in fear that someone, somewhere, had a photograph of him from those early days of Beatlemania. A photograph which could now be shown and used in evidence against him!

Andy had in fact been a fanatical Beatles fan since he'd heard the first wild chords of "Please Please Me" (a song which he earnestly believed had somehow changed his life), following them devoutly through their early singles and first couple of albums; but now as a Mod he'd been forced to accept that, as part of the fierce protocol of what was and wasn't de rigeur listening material, the Beatles were now not cool. Consequently he'd maintained a covert interest in the group - a love, that in those mad, Mod days of the mid-60s, dare not speak its name. It was interesting, to say the least, he thought, how the Beatles were also changing their appearance with the times - McCartney was paying more than lip service to the Mods. Andy reckoned if you looked at the picture of Paul on the front of their "Rubber Soul" LP, already in the shops, and some recent press photos then you could see that McCartney almost had a Mod crop: and he'd read in the music press how McCartney had acknowledged the influence of The Who's unfettered violence on the Beatles' music.

'Come on Andy. Don't hang about!' Don's words jolted Andy from his thoughts as he was offered the use of the wash basin. Don finished his beautification, wiping the last piece of shaving cream from behind his ear as Andy took off his jacket and sports shirt and started to wash. Don and Milt moved across to Laz and the remnants of the Lincoln crowd still in the toilets and engaged them in conversation; from the smiles on their faces and the glances in his direction Andy just knew he was the topic of their conversation. He busied himself in washing and tried to ignore it.

'Hey Andy!' Laz shouted across the room. ' 'heard you made it last night with that bride from Louth.' The room had cleared, with only a dozen or so left in it and the Mod's words echoed mercilessly, reaching everyone there with perfect clarity. They all turned to an already crimson-faced Andy.

'She's always wet and willing.... or so they say - but I wouldn't know about that!' Laz continued.

Andy attempted to diffuse the thrust of the conversation with a dismissive downward wave of his hand.

'First time for the lad.' Don chuckled. Andy was dying silently of embarrassment in front of the mirror.

'Don, wrap up!' he shouted across the room, which was already full of smiles and sniggers.

'Yeah, he's joined the club.' Milt laughed.

'Please!' Andy pleaded. He finished towelling himself dry and put on his sports shirt. He refixed the errant black stripe on his chest and scrutinised himself. What was it with him? - he thought - in the whirl pool of Saturday night sex he'd done what had been expected of him and here he was - still being made to feel about two inches tall. If Andy's romantic tendencies were to be properly served then the details of his loss of virginity and its personal, mystical moments should, more aptly, have been committed to the sanctum of a diary whilst lying in a secret glade, in one of England's broad leafed woodlands, discussed in prose on private pages, beneath the dappled shade of an ancient Oak - not pawed over in public in an underground lavatory in Skegness.

Although the jibes and guffaws had subsided by the time he had rinsed the soap from the basin he still felt he was the subject of some unwelcome conversation.

'How many times d'you do it then Andy?' Don shouted across again, sharing his laughter with the youths around him.

'About 25!' Andy cast a withering look at Don, who naturally ignored it, knowing just how far, and exactly where, to take Andy. It was all part of the ritual in which Milt was also protagonist.

Milt and Don, followed by Laz and a couple of the Lincoln crowd, moved across to Andy and catching him unawares frog marched him to the hot air drier at the foot of the stairs. With the help of the two Lincoln Mods, the four of them hoisted a now struggling Andy to shoulder height, while Laz turned the nozzle from the drier downwards, unzipped Andy's fly and guided the stainless steel nozzle inside his underpants. Laz then banged the "on" button hard with his fist. Amidst the shrieks of laughter, the chanting and clapping of the onlooking Mods and a stream of hot air gusting around his pubic regions, Andy's initiation to consummate manhood was thereby completed.

*

Breakfast at "The Brief" followed. It was the usual Picasso's palette affair - golden crispy toast and butter, burnt ochre beans, yellow and white eggs of the rising sun, over-run with tomato ketchup and all set to music by the juke box.

The three of them joined Laz and the Lincoln crowd and their numbers swelled by the arrival of some of their acquaintances from Stamford and the Sutton scooter lads. No further reference was made to Andy's exploits in the dunes the previous night and seemingly he was now a fully paid-up member of the union.

Someone selected The Byrd's "Mr Tambourine Man" on the juke box and the crystal clear accent of Roger McGuinn reached into the room, bringing America across to the Lincolnshire coast. (Andy preferred Dylan's version of the song - side two, band one, on the "Bringing It All Back Home" album, now deeply etched in memory. The three of them had almost worn out the early Dylan LPs, on Milt's ancient HMV. They had habitually worked on their bikes in the street outside Milt's house with the front door wide open, filling the street with the man's nasal tones. They grooved on all his stuff. Milt's particular favourite was "IT'S ALRIGHT MA, (I'm Only Bleeding)"; Don frequently produced his own version of "Motorpsycho Nitemare" from "Another side"; Andy swore he could see the faces of the penniless miners everytime he heard "NORTH COUNTRY BLUES" from "THE TIMES THEY ARE A-CHANGIN' " album - home from home!)

Much discussion followed on the comparatively new phenomena of Folk Rock, fuelled by The Byrd's rendition of the Dylan song - one of the Stamford lads said "MR TAMBOURINE MAN", by "The Byrds" was the first Folk Rock record. In the lively discussion which followed in "The Brief" Andy kept quiet, taking in all the opinion and counter opinions. He knew what the first Folk Rock song was and it pre-dated "The Byrd's" record by almost 18 months. "Baby Let Me Take You Home", by The Animals was a souped up rock edition of "Baby, Let me Follow You Down" which appeared on Dylan's first album ("I first heard this from Ric Von Schmidt - Ric's a blues guitar player.....").

But The Animals were a greasers' group so Andy kept his opinion to himself; although he liked most of their stuff, from "House of the Rising Sun" onwards, the group had nailed their colours to the mast some months back, when they made their entrance to a "Ready Steady Go!" programme dressed in leathers and riding motorcycles - this was a revelation high on the Richter scale and the after shocks were still ripping through the Mod fraternity.

The slow bass notes of the song's fade-out consigned The Byrds to immediate past history and the selector arm tucked the disc away into the heart of the juke box.

It was a Jingle Jangle Morning.

Someone (Milt estimated their age at about hundred and thirty) selected a Tony Bennett song on the box and there was a collective groan as the song crooned around the café. Andy took in the words of the song; unlike Antonio Bennito, who'd left both right and left ventricles in San Francisco, Andy's heart had been misplaced somewhere in the sand dunes at Skegness.

'Turn this crap off - it's grease music!' a shout went up from the corner of the cafe as "We've Gotta Get Outta This Place" replaced Tony Bennett's ballad. The aggressive voice of Burdon vibrated the speakers. Half way through the song the Mods were reminded of The Animals' choice of sides in the 60s.

'Grease! Grease!' shouted an agitated Mod into the café - 'They're turning your bikes over!', he said, pointing down the road in the direction of the lavatories, where the scooters were parked.

"The Brief Encounter" cafe emptied almost instantaneously. Milt was the first out of the door. Andy was the last. He could see the last of a small raiding party of greasers, riding off in the direction of the prom. Don and Milt were already in pursuit and Andy was left without a mount. He returned to the café as the last few bars of the song were disappearing back into the juke box. He sat down at the table and sipped the remains of his lukewarm tea.

There had always been fights at school (but he tried to avoid them) it was a pastime he never showed any enthusiasm for. As far as the Mod experience was concerned he'd have been happier if everyone just did their own thing - for Andy, the grease were merely peripheral to his life as a Mod. A mere distraction from what he was trying to lift from the 60s and make his own - the clothes, the music and the mood.

He was happy to leave the grease to Milt and also mindful that he hadn't spent the bulk of his recent wage packets on a green gaberdine suit to have it ripped to pieces in a beach fight, by some chain toting individual in jack boots - or worse still have it peed on by some half crazed greaser (now minus his jacket), extracting his revenge for the desecration of his leathers (now rusting in stale urine) the night before.

As he sat alone in the café an added bonus to his present circumstances was that he got to finish his breakfast - which he'd already paid half a crown for.

*

The pursuit of the greasers proved a futile exercise for Milt, Don and the rest of the Mods. Their scooters were no match for the speed of the motor bikes and the leather boys had disappeared northwards into the haze of the morning. Their calling card had been a few slicks of rubber stain, burnt into the warming tarmac and roughly the same number of dents and scratches in the pampered livery of the Mods' scooters. The damage was, in the main, only superficial. Don's fly screen had a hairline crack in it, which now divided the word NEW/ARK and a bent stalk of a wing mirror. Laz's GS had a boot print in one of the chrome side panels and a bent front crash bar.

In an odd way these minor blemishes were already assuming the status of battle scars.

Their anger at this assault on their bikes' bright work had, however, not subsided and the group cruised the town until one of the Lincoln youths from the crow's nest of the last machine in the convoy, spotted a motor cycle and side car combination, parked near the boating lake on the front. A tool kit was strewn on the ground beneath the bike, which was dripping oil from the sump gasket onto the grey tarmac. Three youths in leather's were bent over the machine. They were soon in the middle of the boating lake; having taken the last available boat, in their attempt to evade the group of Mods, Milt, to the fore, running after them through the Crazy Golf Range, vaulting fence and flower beds, in their thirst for revenge.

From the relative safety of the deck of boat number "15" the three motor cyclists viewed the Mods, now only able to chant and jeer from the shore, as the burgeoning police presence, in the shape of three van loads of reinforcements, alerted by local shop keepers and holidaymakers, had mobilised quickly and efficiently and now stood between the Mods and their quarry in the middle of the lake.

Milt had waded into the water but had been yanked out of it after only a couple of paces by one of the policemen. There had been lessons for the learning throughout the summer in the coastal resorts along the eastern and southern fringes of England and the Lincolnshire police now had a complete and practical schooling in dampening down friction between Mods and Rockers.

After the Mods had been persuaded to disperse, the three youths marooned in the boat were escorted to safety and completed their engine repairs under the guard of half a dozen men in uniform and a couple of dogs, thrown in for good measure.

***

SUBSTITUTE

The mid afternoon was hot and oppressive.
The incident at the boating lake had been an isolated one. The hordes of Lincoln Grease had still not shown up. They had heard of a bit of trouble on the beaches of Margate and news was hot that, at Lincoln, the police were turning back train loads of Mods, from Nottingham and Derby, en route for for the resort.

The heat sapped the town's usual busy hum and hustle of its commerce and frantic beach life. It seemed like the whole population was either laying out on the sand or basking on the benches and grass of the pleasure gardens. Ice cream, tea and pop were being consumed in vast quantities, in desperate attempts to lower body temperatures. The donkeys stood motionless on the sand, without patronage, middle-aged men lay motionless, trousers rolled up mid calf length, brows draped with knotted handkerchiefs. Classic. Middle aged women fried - their flesh cooking slowly under the sun. Only the young children displayed their usual boundless supplies of energy, splashing in the sea, which was a gently lapping "bain-marie", slowing heating up this particular edge of England.

Andy, shirtsleeved and sweating, sat on one of the concrete plinths which supported the pier. His green jacket hung from one of the bolt heads securing the barnacle-encrusted girders; although he didn't notice it, the green of the seaweed and algae, which clung to the base of the pier's frame, was the exact colour of his suit. He looked out across the North Sea, over the haze created by the sun's searing heat, doing what he was best at - dreaming.

'If I could choose my place to die it would be somewhere like this....' he said wistfully (his sense of location would, in the fullness of time and travel, ultimately prove to be misplaced). 'I'd just walk out into the sea when my time was up - just keep on walking 'til the ocean swallowed me, and that'd be it....' He paused thoughtfully, 'But knowing my luck I'll

probably peg it at Peterborough.' He screwed up his eyes and squinted. The sun, high and brilliant, coated everywhere and everything in a colour dulling silver/gold veneer. 'Hey, my ship's coming in.' he said, his eyes alighting on the slow, northward movement of a steel ship on the horizon. He paused again, 'Nah, just an empty sampan, heading back to Grimsby!'

The sound of a seagull, shrill and eerie above the beach, distracted him and diverted his daydreaming in another direction. Andy looked upwards to the bird circling above. 'You know,' he said thoughtfully, 'if I could be anything I'd be a seagull - just fly around all day and shit on anybody I wanted.'

He turned around and found Don and Milt had moved away, out of earshot. They were sprawled on the sand, with a group of four girls they'd latched on to in "The Brief" sometime earlier in the day. Three of the girls were heavy Mods, hair cut close to their heads, dark-eyed with mascara and with the same coloured lips. The other girl had classic long, dark hair, steeped in an attitude which was born of pure 60s magazine cover - vague, demure, casual, sophisticated - and devastatingly beautiful. The Mod girls' names were Suze, Denise and Mary; their companion was called Ondine.

None of the three youths had ever met anyone with a name like that; it alone seemed to set her apart from the Mod experience. It was clear she was coming across to them from another world, referenced and defined by her accent and vocabulary.

Denise and Suze had already stripped off down to their bras, while Ondine wore a loose fitting blouse which she had unbuttoned to her navel, allowing the world to gaze in onto the pageant of soft white skin beneath the gently flapping silk. Mary was asleep on Don's lap. The group was seated on a carpet of Parkas, spread over the sand.

Andy walked back to the others, jacket slung over his shoulder and flopped down on the sand beside Ondine. He looked ponderously into her blouse; she made no attempt to conceal her breasts from Andy's stare.

'Jeez I could sink a beer.' Don said shortly, wiping his brow.

'I wanna get blocked.' Milt added.

Andy drew a series of letters in front of him. He sounded as if he'd discovered the secret of the universe in the lexicon in the sand. 'Hey d' you know what the first letters of the ladies' names spells?' he smiled enthusiastically. 'Mary, Ondine, Denise, Suze - ***M.O.D.S.****'*

'Groovy.' said Milt, looking skywards, somewhat less than enthralled.

(A beach, a Bank Holiday, three Mods - united by one lifestyle but divided by thoughts at that particular point in time. Two of them had it in their minds to get high - a Mod's major pre-occupation. Don thought of cold beer. Milt's mind was on French Blues. Andy, rearranging words "into a well known phrase or saying", was thinking of "Sunday Night at the London Palladium", Bruce Forsyth and "Beat the Clock"!)

'Anyway Milt,' Don said casually, 'I thought you had a score or two of Blues - so what's stopping you from getting blocked?'

Milt pulled out a polythene bag, which contained about 30 small tablets, light blue in colour.

'These!' he said, tossing the packet across to Don, who caught it.

Milt had been duped in one of the classic con tricks of the 60s drug culture. It was customary for the conmen of the period to douse Aspirins in blue paraffin in their attempts to pass them off, under dim lights and thick smoke, as French Blue pills. Sometimes it worked. Sometimes it didn't. The vendor who'd taken Milt's money the previous night had shown some concern for the culinary delight of the victim of his tricks - these Aspirins had been soaked in what appeared to be blue calye crystals. Their narcotic effect was zero but they tasted sweet - some people were all heart - Purple Heart.

'Would you recognise the guy who sold 'em to you?' Don asked, tossing the bag back to Milt.

'No, it was dark - but I'd remember the bastard's smell.'

'Excuse me. What's blocked?' the girl Ondine asked Milt.
'It's what Milt said he was gonna be all weekend.' Don reminded Milt, answering the girl's question.
'It's being out of your head - stoked up on pills.' Andy said, smiling at the girl.
'Oh drugs,' she said, 'we got hold of some Cannabis at school awhile back.' Ondine said, 'It was quite - ah - refreshing.'
'Cannabis.' Don dismissed. ' 's an Art School thing - arty farty fumes - 'that right Milt?' he sought Milt's confirmation.

'You can't stay ahead of it on Cannabis.' Milt spoke with the confidence of an authoritarian - 'You need Amphetamine if you're gonna stay awake for an all-nighter down "The Dungeon" or up at "The Wheel" - French Blues....'
'Purple Hearts.' Don added.
'Bombers.' Andy quipped.

'Oh I see.' said Ondine. The youths were more than willing to provide an education.
'Where do you people live?' Ondine continued inquisitively.

'On the streets.' Andy said.
'Anywhere we happen to be.' Don said and stooped to kiss the forehead of the girl Mary, still asleep in his lap.

'Last night it was in a wardrobe in Drummond Road.' Milt said drily, raising titters from Andy.

Ondine was intrigued. The more she was told the less complete seemed her knowledge. 'I'm sorry - a wardrobe?' she looked puzzled.
'It's a long story, ' Milt said, 'I'll tell you later or you can read about it in my memoirs.'

'You can't write can you Milt?' Andy laughed.
'All right clever arse.' Milt responded. 'Ladies, you're looking at Andy - our own private poet laureate - he's saving up to become a nought on "Criss Cross Quiz"!'

Andy shrugged and flashed a smile, which was partly self conscious, partly his acceptance of the way in which he and Milt tore strips off each other from time to time. He looked across at Don and wondered why Don was rarely at the cutting edge of Milt's acerbic tongue, but as Andy spotted the triple stripe on the arm of Don's Parka, just visible underneath Mary's thigh, he knew why - nobody took the piss out of the sergeant, did they?

The girl Ondine fell silent but continued to scrutinise the three youths, as the conversation meandered back and forth amongst them and the two other girls.

'I read in the New Musical Express the other day that the Small Faces are more Mod than The Who.' Andy tossed the sentence into the group.

'Well, Moony's not much of a Mod, with a Beatle cut, is he?' Suze pitched in her two penn'orth.

'Andy, I've told you before. You read too much.' Milt added.

' 's bad for you.' Don laughed.

'They might be more Mod but there're bloody small alright.' Milt said.

'Remember when we saw 'em down "The Dungeon" - or didn't see'em. When they walked on all I could see was a couple of guitars pointing up to the ceiling - and that was it - right through the gig. Machine heads A Go-Go.'

'Yeah, shelled out half a quid - might just as well've been at a bloody disco.' Andy fuelled the conversation.

'But they are good aren't they.' Suze pointed out to Don.

'Oh, they're good alright but it'd be nice to see'em.' Don said smiling.

'Ohhh.... But Roger Daltrey - what I could do for him....' Denise said as her eyes glazed over with lust.

'This Who group - exactly what sort of material do they play?' Ondine asked innocently.

'Jeez sister, where've you been for the last century?' Milt asked her.

'Well actually I've been at finishing school in Switzerland and for the last year I've been at the Sorbonne.' the girl answered. 'I only came back last week.'

Jeez, Andy thought to himself, this was worse than Belloc dying in the 50s - to be alive and beautiful in the mid-60s and **not** *to be in England. Unimaginable.*

'What're you doing on a beach then, with the likes of us?' Don asked her.
'I'm doing a post-grad thesis.' Ondine answered.
'On what?' Andy asked.
'Youth and its tribal behaviour patterns.' Ondine answered.

Andy groaned inwardly - another one who wants to intellectualise us into the sea.

'What were you finishing in Switzerland?' Milt asked casually. The girl Ondine looked puzzled.
'Well it wasn't plaster browning.' Andy butted in.
Milt shrugged. She was out of it. He wished he was out of his head.
***'Dizzy in the head now I'm feeling bad** .....' Milt sang from "'Can't Explain". His hair was the same colour as Daltrey's but his voice bore no resemblance whatsoever.*
'Have you seen them?' Ondine turned to Milt who was, by now, in the song's second verse. Milt nodded but kept on singing.
'Seen'em?' Don said. 'We've got shares in 'em!'
'What about you Suze, Denise?' she said.

'Oh yes,' Suze said, 'three or four times at least - once just before you came back.....'
'Ohhh, Roger Daltrey.....' Denise continued to drool.

Suze foraged in her handbag and pulled out a broken piece of varnished wood with a metal screw thread sticking out of it, the frayed remains of a short length of curled wire were attached to the hole in the metal skewer.
'From "The Barracks" at Grantham - a couple of months back - Pete Townshend's.' Suze handed the remnant of the guitar's machine head to Ondine, who studied the item.
'Yeah, we had to stick it on a couple of tarts from Nottingham, who were after it.' Denise added with pride.

(Standing in front of The Who at Grantham, a month back, Don, Andy and Milt were jammed into a wild crowd of Mods - every one present a part of those transient moments of pop history. There were no cameras, no photographers, no tape recorders, but every note and nuance of that performance was logged in their heads, as indelibly as the images on a reel of film or an album of snapshots, smeared with the thumb prints of the kids who raved there on that night in July.

By its very nature a rock group's live performance is an exercise in the control of its captive audience and yet it can define the individual experience so differently. For Milt, Daltrey was Amphetamine on stage. Don could, at times, match Moon's manic energy and yet there was also an equal affinity with Entwistle, the archetypal bass man - strong and decisive, who anchored the group. Andy, who had forsaken the instrumentals of the Shadows and the likes of the Chantays from the early part of the decade had become a lover of lyrics and tuned into the Modspeak, written by Townshend - the words man, who Andy thought had the most perfect sneer he had ever seen. He appeared almost contemptuous of those he played for and in an odd way it made him even more of an icon.

They'd heard about The Who's recent innovation of smashing instruments in their stage act from some of the Stamford Mods, who'd seen them live at Hitchin, but it wasn't until the Grantham gig that they'd witnessed it for the first time. The group were heavily into their set when the top E string of Townshend's guitar had broken, mid-chord, during one of his vicious arm swinging strikes on the steel string. Within seconds drum sticks were being rammed into speaker baffles, mesh of microphone ripped into skin of snare drum, machine head gouged holes in plaster and paint of the wall behind them - Entwistle played on.

The Who on stage were an aphorism for everyone's latent capacity for violence. Spellbound and agape, they had stood in front of the stage - for this was a microcosm of the Mod, Mod, Mod, mad world.

It was beach fighting. It was parents who couldn't understand. It was the system which couldn't cope - the frustration of kids, who couldn't cope with the system. Anger vented at dirty jobs - at clean jobs, which made you feel dirty. The clamour for Friday night. It was patriotism's last refuge, in a shaped waist jacket, fashioned from the Union Jack. It articulated the unspeakable, glorified the unmentionable, explained the unfathomable.

Like a pilled up Mod, Daltrey had stuttered through "My Generation". He was anybody who was anybody, trying their utmost to cause a big ssssssensation.

And for Andy, the pile of smashed equipment at the end of the show gave form and focus to his despair at having to check 5000 Whitworth nuts and bolts, shoddily produced in a factory's machine shop, dubbed The Mad House.

It was the response to the question Milt would ask himself of Sharon, waiting, swollen and embryonic. Why me? Why me? Why me?)

'Why don't you come up to Leeds next weekend - The Who are playing there.' Suze asked the three of them. 'You could sleep in our shed.'
'Sooner have the wardrobe.' Milt observed.
'Ritz, man.' Don quipped.

Ondine continued to roll the machine head fragment around in her palm. Milt yawned and shielded his eyes from the sun, which was starting its journey homeward over the Lincolnshire Wolds.

' 'you bored Milt?' Don asked.
'Yeah, I'm bored, I should be blocked and instead I'm baking.'
' 'you bored Andy?' Don enquired.
Andy shook his head. The last time he had experienced terminal boredom was in a double period of Latin on a Thursday afternoon in 1963.
'What about you ladies?' The question was answered with smiles and shrugs.

'What d'you wanna do Milt?' Don asked him.
'Well, first we mine the beach, then we dynamite the pier.....' he suggested drily. Don laughed.
' 'fancy a game then?' Don asked mischievously.

'What sort of a game Donny boy?' Milt looked puzzled.
'Oh, nothing too spectacular,' Don said, 'sort of a treasure hunt, right.'
'What, dredging the Wash for King John's treasure?' Andy asked, smiling.
'O.K. what's the crack?' Milt asked.
'Well - in an hour you have to bring back an object - which I choose.' Don said, smiling.
'We used to do that in the Scouts.' Andy said seriously.
'You and those frigging Scouts!' Milt rounded on Andy, 'Load of prats - Brown Owl and all that crap!'
'That's Brownies, prat.' Andy said.

'Anyhow,' Milt said, turning back to Don, 'what object?'
'Well Milt,' Don said and then paused for a while, 'for you - a Greaser's helmet.'

Milt started to laugh dismissively. 'Hey man, you're putting me on.' he said.
Don smiled, as did the girls and Andy. The smile soon left Andy's face after Don spoke again.
'Andy - you can bring us a ten bob note.'
'Ten bob!' Andy shouted, 'where I am I going to get ten bob.'
'Use your initiative.' Don smiled.
'Yeah, like you do in the Scouts and the Duke of Edinburgh's.' Milt added sarcastically.

Milt and Andy were silent, contemplating Don's proposals.
'It could be interesting,' Ondine broke the silence, 'we all evolved from hunter/gatherers.'
'You what?' Milt said, smiling thinly.

The girl tossed Townshend's guitar fragment back to Suze - 'Suze has her trophy, yours would be the helmet.'

Milt pondered for a while. 'And what about you Donald?' Milt made a point of addressing his friend with his full name - a practice he knew infuriated Don.

Don bristled momentarily but quickly shrugged off his prickliness.
'Well, I thought for me a pair of ladies' knickers.' He stroked the forehead of the girl in his lap, who was just beginning to emerge from her siesta. 'Or perhaps a bra.'

'Yeah, bloody typical,' Milt said softly, 'why is it you're calling the tune?'
'Rank, mate!' Don said smiling, pointing to the three stripes on the sleeve of his Parka.
'I bet you couldn't get one Milt.' the girl Ondine said.
'I could get a dozen sister, but I don't feel like it.' Milt responded.
'Oh go on Milt,' Denise joined in the cajoling process, 'show us what you can do.'
'Yes, come on Milt.' Suze urged. 'Just one greaser's crash hat.'
Milt was under mounting pressure to provide the sport in this distraction of the hot afternoon. Pressure from peers - wasn't that the motive force which powered the Mod machine?
'O.K.,' he said, getting up from the sand, 'you're on,' and smiling as he started to walk away across the beach, he added confidently, 'd'you want a bike as well?'

*

Half an hour after leaving the beach Milt was no nearer his allotted task - where were the hordes of Lincoln grease? he thought, as he wandered aimlessly around the town, must've scared them off, he mused. He was beginning to believe his own myths. There were plenty of Mods, cruising around on their scooters, trying to diffuse the heat, which was still slowly baking the town.
The police presence had steadily increased, anticipating the trouble which so far hadn't materialised - they were all dressed in summer garb, having discarded their jackets. Two of them, patrolling on foot, passed Milt as he walked down towards the railway station. He caught the whiff of their body odour coming off the damp patches of sweat, spreading out slowly from beneath their armpits and logged up in his head that the colour of their light blue shirts would tone in perfectly with his faded Levis.
Jeez, what am I doing here? he thought.
In another part of town a juke box in a café filled the air with music. The brief introductory guitar riff was followed by the first words of the song.

"You think we look pretty good together"

Come on, he thought, just one lousy greaser's helmet, I'm not asking for the world.

He passed the shop with barely a second glance on his way down the street. Five minutes later he was standing on the opposite side of the road, staring at the display in its window.

"You think my shoes are made of leather"

Milt looked around furtively and crossed over the road. He glanced again into the window and turned his back to the plate glass front as a customer, clutching a paper bag containing his purchase, came out into the street. He pushed past Milt, who stood looking down into the gutter, the sole of his boot nervously tapping the kerb stones. With a last check, as to who was in the street, he entered the shop.

"But I'm a substitute for another guy
I look pretty tall but my heels are high"

'How much is the red crash hat in the front of the window please?' Milt asked the shop keeper. The man was silent for a time, eyeing Milt from head to desert boots.

' 'didn't think your lot wore crash hats.' His knowledge of the Mods was born from the experience of two seasons of high summer mayhem and the replacement of at least one shop front as a result of it.

'How much?' Milt persisted.

"The simple things you see are all complicated"

'Three pounds ten.' the shop keeper said, placing both hands with arms outstretched on the glass counter cabinet, almost daring Milt to buy it.

"I look pretty young but I'm just back-dated"

' 'you got anything cheaper?' Milt enquired, looking around the shop, particularly at the door.

"Substitute!"

' 'depends how much you value your brains,' the man said tersely and as Milt turned to the sound of the bell on the door, he muttered underneath his breath, ' not many of yours to the pound, I bet.'

Milt turned back to the man as the person, who had opened the door, thought twice and closed it, without entering the shop.
'Well have you?' Milt pressed the man.

"I see right through your plastic mac"

'This one's two pounds seven and six.' the man said, removing a greyish, green crash hat from the counter cabinet and handing it to Milt.
'Wouldn't have thought it was your colour though.' he added sarcastictly. He could take or leave Milt's custom.

Milt took the hat gingerly and held it by its strap, unwilling to touch it more than was absolutely necessary.
'I'll take it.' he said. Milt went out into the street, just as stealthily as he had left it.

"I look all white but my dad was black...."

Milt walked quickly away from the shop in the direction of the beach, his newly acquired head gear wrapped up in a paper bag and wedged tightly under his arm, as far out of sight as possible.

'Milt! Milt!' he heard a female voice shouting to him and turned in the direction of the sound. Across the street, a young girl, aged about fourteen, was waving wildly, 'Milt! Milt!' she shouted

Milt stopped as the girl ran across the road with blind disregard for the traffic, followed by her two female companians.

'Jeez, Zoob the Pube.' Milt said softly to himself and shortly she was by his side. Her stature was such that her head was at the level of Milt's armpit, presently filled with crash hat. She besieged Milt's space as she bounced around the pavement with her companions.

'Milt, where have you been all weekend, I've been looking for you all over?'

'I know.' Milt's words were loaded with the weight of his friends' jibes during the weekend. (Maureen, the raver from Sheffield, was enthusiasm A Go-Go, most of it channelled in Milt's direction. She had snapped on to him since he had unwisely engaged her in conversation, one Saturday night at "The Mojo", a couple of months back. It had been dark in the club - (that was Milt's excuse). Her uncle was a DJ at Stringfellow's establishment, on the road to Rotherham.

Maureen, the undisputed queen of catalogue shopping chic, was a season out of time with the clothes she wore and as many months behind in music as Andy was in payments for his bike. She was hot when she should have been cool - loud when quietness was called for - moved, when she should have been still - and, so she had convinced herself in her pubescent confusion, madly in love with Milt. Her heart, however, was in the right place. At this moment in her life it was beneath her see-through plastic mac, which had steamed up in the afternoon's heat, with its inside surface covered in globules of condensation - some of which had already started to move in a slow southward trickle en route to the bottom of the garment. They joined the collected moisture now starting to drip from the hem onto the pavement.)

'How long've you been down?' Maureen bubbled.

'Since Saturday.' Milt answered cagily, looking around, embarrassed.

'I wonder why I haven't seen you sooner.'

'Can't imagine.' Milt added drily.

'Take me to the disco tonight Milt.'

'No chance sister!' Milt replied emphatically.

'Oh, why not Milt - please!' she persisted, 'why not!'

' 'cos I've turned Greaser baby.' Milt, surprising himself at his quickness of wit, pulled the crash hat from its bag and thrust it towards Maureen and her two companions. They flinched and moved one step backwards. 'Oh no Milt, you can't have!' Maureen's voice conveyed genuine despair.

'I can ***and*** *have - now I ride a Bonneville and own a Brylcreem factory!' Milt launched into what he perceived as a perfect escape route from Maureen's worst excesses. Plausible enough to provide permanent refuge.*

'Oh Milt - no!'

'Oh yes Milt - from now on you will call me Agostini.'

'Laz said you'd been asking after me - oh Milt you can't turn greaser. I won't let you.....' She put her hand on Milt's arm only to be repelled by a further thrust of the crash hat. (Milt was beginning to think this was probably the best two pounds seven and sixpence he'd ever spent.)

'Too late baby - I'm even renouncing pills.' Milt said, pulling out the pack of duff French Blues he'd been conned into buying last night. He handed the polythene bag to Maureen. It rested in the palm of her hand while she and her friends examined it.

'A small parting present,' Milt added, 'something to help you over the shock of never seeing me again.'

'Oh Milt,' Maureen said, dewy eyed, touched. She carefully opened up the loosely tied polythene bag.

'They're specials baby - real mind blowers.' Milt said secretively and quietly.

'What are they?' Maureen asked.

'They're called Aspirinozos.' Milt said, turning away momentarily to stifle a grin.

'Do I swallow them whole?' Maureen asked, taking a couple of the pills from the bag.

'No, you stuff'em in your ears.' Milt added curtly, ' 'course you swallow 'em - go on!'

Maureen hesitated.

'Go on - take a few. Get outta your head!' Milt urged.

Maureen put three or four of the tablets into her mouth, gulping each one down.

'Oh...er... Milt,' she said, with saliva restored to her throat, 'they're good, aren't they?...oh.....er....I'm high! I'm high! It's fantastic isn't it?'
'It's them thar Aspirinozos baby.' Milt said smiling.
'I'm high! I'm high!....Stoned! I'm stoned!'
With those parting words Maureen and her two young friends bounced away along the pavement in the opposite direction to Milt's resumed journey back to the beach.

*

Half way down the road Milt ducked into an alleyway, dividing a rock shop and an ice-cream kiosk. He made his way down between the buildings and then stopped, pulling the crash hat out of its bag. He ripped off the price tag and quality inspection stickers from the helmet and discarded them, along with the polythene covering. Taking a handful of soil, gravel and loose stones he rubbed them roughly into the black leather lining to the hat and then emptied them out, leaving some of the dirt clinging to the natural lines in the surface of the leather. He threaded the free end of the chin strap through the buckle and fastened it on the middle hole of the strap; taking firm hold of the leather either side of the buckle, he yanked hard three or four times, leaving an elongated oval hole in place of the newly punched circular perforation. With both hands tightly gripping the ear pieces he smashed it on the rough surface of the alleyway - the loose grit and gravel bit into the highly polished surface, scuffing and denting it, disguising its shiny newness. After half a dozen similar operations the crash hat was instantly antique and looked as if it had been worn by some skid lid kid for years, providing the means of survival in countless crashes.

Milt was about to leave the alley when he was distracted by muffled sounds coming from the small yard at the end of the wall on the left. He walked further down the narrow pathway and caught the sight of a figure wearing a black leather jacket and calf length boots, fastened from instep to knee by black straps and buckles. He intervened quickly when he saw a Mod youth, in the familiar attire of the period, slowing getting his face and clothes re-arranged at the hands and feet of two stray greasers.

Dropping the crash hat, Milt dived into the fight and the extra help he provided quickly evened up the one-sided affair it had been, before his arrival. Before too long the two black clad youths, satisfied with the damage they had managed to inflict on the two Mods, sloped off down the alley, leaving Milt with blood trickling from a cut lip and his clothes in disarray.

Milt sat down with his back against one of the brick walls which formed the yard, catching his breath and repairing the ravages to his hair and clothing. He looked across to the other Mod, who had lain motionless, but now showed signs of movement, as he slowly raised himself from his prone position.

When this other youth had wiped away the blood which had run from his nose, smearing his face, they stared at each other in mutual recognition. Milt looked on to the now blotchy features of "The Smiler" - those fists, used by the youth in his defence a few minutes ago, were formed by the same fingers which had undone the fixing bolts to the back rack of Milt's Vespa, a few months back.

The back rack now for sale, in a caravan at Ingoldmells.

'You bastard!' Milt coughed. 'I should've left you to the Grease.' Milt was dazed, confused. Tribal protocol had forced him to render assistance to one of his number. Would Milt's actions have been any different if he had known who he was actually helping? - probably not, and that knowledge was the root of Milt's anger.

'I'm sorry about your back rack.' "The Smiler" spluttered words coated in blood, 'I'll get you another.'

'Piss off!' said Milt gathering up the crash helmet. He walked slowly from the alleyway into the street, leaving "The Smiler" rubbing his bruises.

In a matter of minutes Milt had made it back to Don, Andy and the girls on the beach. He made a great show of wiping away a smidgen of congealed blood from the corner of his mouth, sucking the last remnant of red into his mouth and stood there smiling broadly, swinging the crash hat to and fro in his fingers.

He eventually let go of it. It thudded into the sand in front of Don. 'Piece of cake!'

***

THE COME DOWN

BRINGING IT ALL BACK HOME

In the 60s, thousands of people it seemed went to work on an egg.

On the Tuesday morning after the weekend Andy went to work on the back of Don's scooter. The three of them had ridden through the Monday night and early Tuesday morning in a desperate attempt to wring the last precious moments of life out of the Bank Holiday. They had travelled back with some of the Stamford crowd and a quartet of kids from Peterborough, passing through Boston, dominated by the illuminated presence of The Stump, reaching skywards from the heart of the fen, and along the flat, dyke lined, Lincolnshire roads to Donnington.

The Stamford crowd peeled off southwards at the Threekingham turn, shouting and waving their goodbyes, as Don, Milt and Andy maintained their westward course: through the last reaches of Billingborough Fen, Dembleby Thorns, Heydour and Ropsley Heath, intersected by The Long Hollow and the other Roman Roads which divided up their journey like the design of a giant mosaic. They crossed the Ley lines of the county, their home bound run backlit by a full, blue moon.

They reached Grantham as dawn was beginning to break and were alone as they sped down Spittlegate Hill, past the RAF base, ringed with barbed wire, with its fighter plane, displayed in full combat colours, on the neatly clipped grass at the entrance gates to the airfield.

The air, forced out from beneath their bikes and through the chain-link perimeter fencing of the air base, created a soft whistling sound as they passed, which underscored the engine notes of the Lambretta and Vespa, the cool morning air providing the perfect conditions for the carburation of the fuel mixture. Rounding the corner of the bottom of the hill, they were soon moving along St Peter's Hill - deserted. Tollemache's statue at the head of the park welcomed them into the town, where so many of the stories of their lives as Mods had been written; the bronze form of Isaac Newton, set high on a stone plinth in front of the Guild Hall, towered over the slatted bench which wound itself around the statue. This had been one of their designated meeting places, on which the three of them had spent a good part of their time in the town, sitting or sleeping, either waiting for women, or each other and occasionally, in Milt's case, oblivion.

Out, up and over Gonerby Hill, they coasted into Tony's Transport Cafe, nestling at the hill foot on the Great North Road, which now by-passed the town. The car park was empty, save for a handful of lorries parked up for the night, the drivers asleep in their cabs. They were served by the mother of one of the girls they knew from Grantham who gave them steaming hot tea in pint mugs, usually reserved for the lorry drivers only. They were silent as they sipped their tea and contemplated the week of day-shift drudgery which lay in front of them. It had been a hell of a weekend. The only tenuous connection between this work-a-day Tuesday morning and their few crazy days out on the coast was the sun, now rising quickly and quietly over Loveden Hill, promising a swelter to match the dog day heat in which the Bank Holiday had smouldered.

They finished their tea and fell asleep, collapsed over table and chairs, exhausted as the weekend finally expired, carried away from them by the traffic lumbering northwards on that Great North Road.

They were awakened as the cleaning staff clambered around them in their morning process of cleaning the floor; this consisted of giving the room what amounted to a strip wash - clearing one half of the floor of tables and chairs and scrubbing the exposed tiles clean with detergent and disinfectant The process was then repeated on the other half of the room - unfortunately, this now contained the sleeping trio. The clock on the front wall was showing 5.45 am as they were prodded into life by the mops and brush handles of a handful of giggling, overalled girls.

Outside in the car park the noise of the lorries heading north brought them back in touch with the reality of their day jobs and presently they embarked on the last fifteen miles of their journey; for the first time in four days they felt anonymous, invisible and alone in the streams of traffic being simultaneously spewed around England.

*

The Tuesday at work was, for Andy, a nightmare.

By the time he had clocked in at the time office, the factory was already working. His late arrival by eight minutes would result in half an hour's pay being docked and his lateness prompted the usual collective ritual of being "banged in" to his work area on the checking slab which, as fate would have it, was sited at the far end of the machine shop; as he walked down the centre aisle, flanked each side by lathes, his tardy arrival was announced by the whole shop, to a man (and boy) banging loudly with spanners, chuck keys, iron bars, wrenches on anything that would make a noise - oil drums, machine guards, conveyor rollers and the cast iron standings of the machines. Andy, sleeping bag under one arm and with his Parka swung over the other, walked briskly past the cheering, banging and jeering boiler-suited operatives. The cacophony of noise stopped only when he reached the other end of the shop. He thereby swapped the fresh smell and the sounds of the sea for the insane din of metal hammering on metal and the acrid stench of the industrial swarf of Machine Shop 'A' - The Mad House.

He changed out of his suit, hanging it on a peg on the wall behind the checking slab - it was in dire need of a good press up when he could finally get it home later; like him, it had been through a lot in the last few days.

He worked silently, sullenly, wearing only his underpants beneath the blue twill boilersuit - the heat in the building increasing steadily with the August sun beating on the north lighted roof, and the warmth generated by the combined revolutions of numerous spindle lathes.

He had spent the morning checking the last of the five thousand 3/8th" Whitworth nuts and bolts - a job he had been occupied with for over a week - in the words of Mr. Polly from the Wells book, which he had studied for '0' level, this was simply "**boredom indescribable**".

His time on the checking slab had followed stints in other parts of the factory - Steam, Monobloc and Centrifugal Pump Shops and Millwrights - these planned movements around the factory were all part of a programme to enable him to gain a variety of experience in a technical apprenticeship which would eventually lead him to a position on the technical sales force and the prospects of earning some real money; as he plugged away, testing each nut and bolt with the gauges, not even the thoughts of an improvement in his financial status could dispel the feeling that, after nearly a year at the place, he was a round peg in a square hole.

On this Tuesday morning at the checking slab he had re-focused himself and in those few hours of almost robotic work he had come to the conclusion (which he should have reached months ago - if only then he had put some thought into it) - this job was driving him crazy. He drifted into it and now he wanted out of it - of that he was convinced. The problem was only one of ***how*** and not ***why.*** Maybe it was the weekend and all it now signified, which had brought him to his senses. His indifference to literature at school had, in his year out, now been supplanted by almost a yearning for it - but not a literary critical exposition - the like of which lay in all the Notes. He just wanted the words - the words as they appeared on the pages of the novels, plays and poems. Sitting at the slab he concluded that engineering and its religion of fine clearances in machining metal, required no more precise a skill than a novelist, poet or playwright employed, working with the fine tolerances of words.

He was congratulating himself on this, his astounding piece of brainwork of the morning, when reality arrived in the shape of another steel box of Whitworth nuts, which Harry, his immediate superior, dragged from beneath the slab. Andy's jaw dropped at the sight of hordes of even more brass hexagons.

''don't want you getting bored Andy,' Harry smiled. 'These should be a bit more interesting.'

'Interesting!' Andy croaked, staring at the nuts.

'Yes - why not?' Harry asked.

'I've just checked 5,000.' Andy protested.

'What size?' Harry enquired.

'3/8ths.' Andy answered softly.

'Well, that's it - these are ½" - much more interesting.' Harry laughed while Andy gazed woefully on his next job.

'How many are there?' Andy asked.

'Oh, only 6,000.' Harry said casually.

'And I've got to check 'em all?' Andy protested again.

'No, 'course not Andy,' Harry consoled. 'just every other one!'

*

Don's Tuesday morning had ultimately taken on a different perspective than he had originally envisaged. Unable to face a day of crawling around underneath the new multi-tubular boiler or in the roof void of Staythorpe "B" Power Station's boiler room extension, choking on the fibres of insulating material, he decided to call in sick - (unlike Andy, he could cope with pay being docked, earning more in a day than Andy did in a week) - after all, he had, in his last year at school, turned truancy into an art form, so why, he thought, on this glorious summer day which beckoned, change the habits of a lifetime? As befit his rank as the unofficial leader of the pack he transformed his day into a more laid back and leisurely affair than the one which Andy, sweating under his overalls, found himself locked into at the pump factory.

Don spent the morning topping up his suntan while he cleaned the Lambretta and repaired the minor dents in the machine's paintwork, also straightening those parts of the scooter's chrome accessories bent in their skirmish with the Grease on the Sunday morning.

His dad was at work and the note his mother had written, told him that she was staying over at her sister Mavis's for the rest of the week. Don's mother had been there, consoling his aunt, since Bert's funeral on the Saturday.

*

Don sat on a now gleaming Lambretta Rally Master, waiting for Maggie outside the corset factory where she worked. She got off early on Tuesdays and was full of her weekend in London with Phil, the Mod from Peterborough. Don listened in silence as they rode through Newark en route to his house.

With the house to himself they spent the afternoon making love.
The level of privacy Don usually enjoyed when he entertained girls with his parents around was restricted to the confines of his bedroom, with a chair stuck under the door handle; on this afternoon they did it all over the semi-detached dwelling and, in the words of his mother (as she threw herself into her annual spring cleaning) gave each room a "thorough going over".

They shook windows and rattled walls: and within a short space of time it became abundantly clear that Don and Maggie's version of a "thorough going over" bore little resemblance to Mrs Hadden's fastidious attitude to the welfare of carpets and upholstery.

*

Milt had travelled homewards along London Road as Don and Andy had peeled off down the road to the factory where Andy worked. The town was just starting to come to life, warming gently in the sun's first rays. He passed crowds of overalled workers pedalling in both directions - some on their way to the pump factory, where Andy had just been deposited and the opposite flow of cyclists homing in on the ball-bearing manufacturers, at the other end of the town.

These two factories provided the bulk of the employment for the towns' people - the place revolved around the works, like the moon of some lost planet. Everyone in the town knew someone who worked at Worthington Simpson or Ransome & Marles. The factories had a strangle hold on Newark, as tight as that of the mines on the pit villages in the north of the county; the delicate industrial balance of the place was thus created in the ambivalence of its workers. The town came to a virtual standstill during the two weeks of their annual shut down, when it emptied itself of over half its population who, for a fortnight, sought respite from the rigours of these twin task masters and their quest for excellence through engineering and ingenuity.

One of the cyclists called his name as Milt braked, swerving to avoid a cat darting across the road from behind a parked milk float. Milt turned to the sound, but his speed prevented him from putting a name to the voice. This shouted salutation from the group of workers on their way to "clock-on" reminded him of the work days which lay before him. He wished he could just turn himself around, then and there and reclaim what he had left behind on the coast. In contrast, the crash hat, purchased in desperation at Skegness, was fastened to the Vespa's front rack by its chin strap and rocked gently against the chrome tubes of the frame - a symbol of what he was in fact bringing back with him - contradiction born of compulsion.

He turned off the main road in the last few hundred yards of his journey and entered his street. Oddly, he negotiated the corner in what was, for him, an orderly fashion. No sparks from the bike's undercarriage on the raised manhole cover in the street. No screech of tyres. No breaking away of the rear end of the GS in his usual controlled skid. He eased slowly over to the right hand side of the street and then turned into the left, to approach the entrance to his terrace at right angles. He mounted the pavement by way of the wooden ramp he had constructed and left in the gutter, against the kerb. The front suspension dipped and re-bounded as he entered the passageway.

The sound of the Vespa's engine changed its tone as it reverberated along the engineering bricks which formed the passageway's floor. It was dark inside and there couldn't have been more than a few thou between the external dimensions of the bike and its chromium plated accoutrements, in the shape of mirrors and flags; but, like a cat relying on its whiskers and a butterfly on its sonic radar, Milt prided himself that whenever he had negotiated this passage way on his bike he had never scraped the brickwork or had to remove his feet from the running boards as a result of poor bikemanship.

There had been times on his early morning homecomings when he'd met his dad or Stan, his next door neighbour, leaving for work on Ransomes' early shift and on his late night arrivals he had been known to disturb Stan's daughter snogging passionately (or petting heavily) with the latest boyfriend; on these occasions collision had been averted and decorum preserved as a result of emergency action - by Milt placing his foot to the floor and Stan's daughter putting herself back into her underwear.

He rounded the corner at the end of the passage and killed the engine. He dismounted and wheeled the bike towards the shed at the side of the garden. He set the scooter on its stand and opened the door of the shed.

Sharon was waiting for him.

''llo Milt.' She said softly,' 'good weekend?'

Milt was surprised and phased by her presence. He had succeeded at the weekend in obliterating all thoughts of her.

'Yeah, not bad ...' he spoke quickly, deliberately, almost without drawing breath. He knew what the drift of the conversation would be when he paused.

He would have talked all his life if it could stave off the inevitable.

'Bit of a snore at times though.

You dare to look me in the eye,

Some of the Peterborough crowd were there - and the Sutton scooter lads.

Crocodile tears are what you cry,

Not a bad party though on Saturday night -

And a genuine problem you won't try,

Wrecked the bloody joint ....

To work it out at all - just pass it by,

The law nearly tabbed us ....'

Pass it by.

Sharon listened without speaking and then started to cry. The sobs, which filled her eyes with tears, were separated by the deep breaths she was forced to take to sustain them.

'Sharon, hey Sharon.' Milt put his arm around her. Grains of sand which had been concealed within the cuff of his Parka spilled on to her shoulder and formed a speckled pattern on the dark fabric of her coat.

'Don't cry Sharon,' he said, looking around to see if their conversation had an audience in the form of parents or neighbours, 'it'll be OK.'

Words, just words. Worthless words. Words which had absolutely no meaning.

'Milt how can you say that!' Sharon called on inner strengths - anger replacing tears. 'It's not going to go away is it? It's going to get bigger and bigger and it's your's Milt.' She started to cry again, 'Milt, I'm going to have your baby. Don't you understand?'

Milt moved away down the garden, to give himself some space. He padded up and down the earth path between the flowers growing in profusion on the one side - crimson Salvias, Stocks (their perfume faded now) the muted shades of Love-in-a-Mist, Michaelmas Daisies ready to burst - and on the other, the neat rows of vegetables - Lettuce, Radish, Beetroot, Cabbages, divided by weedless margins of finely tilled soil - tilth created by the sharp blade of spade, rake and hoe, the results of his father's painstaking horticultural care.

The long garden was a suburban temple, celebrating life from seed to bloom and fruit. Milt had hardly given the garden a second glance for at least a couple of years. The last time he had walked up it as far as the spot where he now stood, staring at the vegetables covered in dew, was last summer when he and Andy had purloined the remains of the chromium framework of an old pram, rotting in the bottom shed; these were now incorporated as the supports for the backrest on Don's Lambretta.

The fecundity of the garden now seemed inescapable, conspiratorial almost. His seed growing within Sharon; silent, inevitable, as the vertical and linear thrust of the plants. He turned and walked back towards her, catching sight of his mother, as she opened the back bedroom curtains, then melting back into the room away from the window.

'Oh Milt, what 're we going to do?' Sharon pleaded. It was however, only rhetoric born of desperation. There were, she knew, only two options, two ways to solve the equation. To have it or not to have it.

'Oh shit! shit!' Milt said, 'I don't know, I can't think - I've just ridden from Skeg - I've been up half the night - I'm knackered - shit! - I don't know.'
'Well you'd better start thinking.'
'Me! Me! Is it all my fault?' He sounded hopeless. She stared at him, saying nothing, allowing his words to gain weight in the brief silence.
'I've got to get to work.' She said, trying to compose herself, wiping her eyes.
'I'll see you tonight - can you pick me up? - please?'
Milt nodded and watched her walk down the garden and down the passageway. She walked without looking back. He went into the shed and fiddled around with the paraphernalia in it - aimlessly picking up and putting down, feeling the weight in the spanners and sockets on the bench, squeezing sponges. Preoccupied. Pensive.
''thought you'd forgotten where you live.' The words of his mother, standing at the door of the shed, jolted him from his thoughts.

(Whydontchaallfffffffffff......)

''Have a good time then?' She asked him. He smiled. 'Was that Sharon I've just seen?' He nodded in silence. ''cat got your tongue?' She enquired.
'No I'm just tired.' He said.
'Is Sharon alright Peter?' His mother asked.

He turned his face away.

*

Andy had no stomach for either the 6,000 ½" Whitworth Nuts, which lay in wait as his next job, or the tomato sandwich he had been obliged to cadge for his lunch from one of the lads in The Madhouse. He had spent up (surprise!) at Skegness and was left without even the two shillings required to purchase the subsidised "dish of the day" at the works' canteen. He wished his scrounged lunch had been anything other than a tomato sandwich: while still at school he once mentioned to his mother that he quite liked them and accordingly got them daily in his pack-up for the next two years.

Most of his fellow workers in the Machine Shop, who didn't patronize the canteen and its rare brand of cordon bleu cuisine, ate their packed lunches while sitting on the floor behind the lathes, backs against the outer wall of the shop.

Andy usually liked to get some fresh air in his mid-day break, occasionally accepting a lift into Newark town or to the pub in Balderton village, but usually walking the perimeter of the factory site and ending up at the far end of the complex, where the offices stood. It was here that the majority of the office girls, including some of the Mod girls he knew, spent their lunchtimes in summer on the lawns and patios. The sight of firm breasted, long legged members of the opposite sex, stretched out in the noon day sun, was altogether more appealing to the sensual side of his nature than sitting on the concrete footings of the machinery, rubbing shoulders with boiler suited apprentices, all up to their arm pits in machine oil, covered in gun metal grey sequins of mild steel turnings and rhinestones of powdered swarf, waiting for the factory hooter and the start of the afternoon shift.

Today was different - he was too knackered and too depressed at the passing of the weekend (and what he now had in its stead) that not even sunshine on sallow female skin could motivate him; it may have been post coital triste, mental (or metal) fatigue or just plain apathy, but he just didn't have the wherewithal. He spent the lunchtime with his backside chilling on cold concrete, wedged in the long blue line of his compatriots in The Madhouse, having feasted on his tomato sandwich, washed down by half a bottle of milk, in a state of anaesthesia, staring at the cast iron base of a turret lathe for the best part of an hour - probably the same piece of ironmongery which was responsible for the manufacture of the thousands of Whitworth nuts which awaited him at the checking slab.

Machine Shop 'A', nicknamed The Madhouse, was populated by an army of apprentices being taught the rudiments of machine turning - some of the kids he was now sitting alongside still had no idea of even the most basic facets of the job and virtually everything which came off their machines went straight into the scrap box: anything which looked half decent went to Andy's checking slab for him to test against the fine tolerances demanded by the industry.

He sat motionless, eyes half glazed and although he didn't notice it, the green of the lathe's footing, immediately in front of him, was the exact colour of his suit, now hanging in his locker and like himself at that moment, sadly in need of a press and freshening up.

At about 1.00 pm the factory hooter sounded and, almost robot like, the thin blue line rose and made its way back to the lathes.

The muted atmosphere of the shop, silent in its break, was soon shattered as, one by one, the lathes were started up and the hum of the motors, spinning chucks and the splatter of coolant against the splash backs to the machines, filled the shop with the clatter and rattle of the light engineer, from concrete foundation to the north-lighted roof space.

Andy hated the lunchtime hooter in the same way as he had, in his last few months at school, come to detest the sound of the school bell ringing out over the quad at the end of the dinner break period. It seemed that whole chunks of his life were for ever being divided up by bells and hooters.

For whom the bell tolls, it tolleth for thee, Andrew.

Andy remained seated for a short time until he was fetched by Harry, his boss, and received a mild bollocking for his time keeping. He "clocked on" for the afternoon by banging his time card in the clocking in machine just before its print stamp went over on to red (and into the dreaded realms of wage deductions).

He looked at the box of nuts and scooped up handfuls of them, letting them drop through his fingers back into the box: how he wished it was the soft sand from Anderby Creek cascading between his fingers.

''won't get done by looking at them Andy!' Harry shouted across to him.

'Have you got the ½" Whit screw gauge?' Andy asked Harry, who checked his tool box and his work area on the slab.

'No, you'll have to get it from the tool room over at Number '1'. Harry replied.

Andy smiled, grateful for any small gift of a time waste which might divert him from the job. With any luck it might be a quarter of an hour before he got back.

'Have you got your checks?' Harry asked earnestly. Andy fumbled into his breast pocket and pulled out a round brass disc with a hole punched into the top near its rim and with his "clocking in" number stamped on both of the polished faces of the disc.

'Yep!' Andy replied, tossing the tool check in the air like a coin. He missed catching it as it came down from above his head and rolled under the slab at Harry's feet.

'Now I've told you Andy - keep your checks safe and don't play around with them.' Harry admonished Andy as he handed him the tool check.

'Yeah.' Andy quipped as he set off from the Machine Shop on his way to the tool room.

The double doors to Machine Shop Number 1, which housed the tool room, were wide open in an attempt to let some air into the large building, whose ambient temperature was of oven like intensity. The building was twice the size of The Madhouse, having a more diverse concentration of machinery (and shook with about double the level of noise). On his way to the tool room Andy walked past rows of capstan lathes, hydraulic power presses, vertical drillers, Cincinatti millers, shaping machines and the huge degreasing plant - he winced as the smell of the hot ether solution drifted into his nostrils - jeez, he thought, this was probably what hell would smell like.

This was the pits.

He stopped just before the tool room, which had a queue in front of it and watched a man, immaculately attired in a freshly pressed overall, with hardly a spot of oil or grease on it, polishing the steel parts of a lathe with a duster. All around him, down the aisles of whirring machinery, the operatives were busy on Piece Work, grafting flat out to bolster their wage packets with their own and their share of the shop's collective bonus; this man, however, was more concerned with the cleanliness of his machine. Andy gazed on, fascinated and yet saddened by the spectacle. It was hard for him to comprehend why someone would want to polish a turning machine - a Vespa's side panels maybe, but not a Colchester spindle lathe!

The man turned around, sensing Andy's stare.

''looking good Fred.' Andy said humouring the man, who was one of the characters of Machine Shop Number 1; he had already put in 40 years - straight from school. Andy baulked at that much time spent in a place like this. Christ, how many times must he have heard the bloody hooter!

'Sure is Jimmy. Always keep her in trim.' the man answered, returning quickly to his buffing. The paintwork on the machine fair gleamed.

'Fred - my name's Andy!'

'Sure it is Jimmy.' Fred answered.

'Must be the cleanest machine in Number 1.' Andy said, glancing back at the tool room, whose queue had now virtually cleared.

'No doubt about it Jimmy. She's the queen of the shop!' Fred said, putting the duster on his stool and picking up his chuck key, he walked around the machine to the stock of steel rods, racked up on a roller fed metal storage system and started to pull one out.

With Fred out of sight Andy produced a mouthful of saliva, spat it on the shiny gun metal paint on the base of Fred's machine and then walked up to the tool room window. The man in the tool room looked down on Andy. 'Have you got the ½" Whit screw gauge please?' Andy asked him, rattling a couple of his tool checks in his palm. The man looked at the large peg board which covered the whole of the back wall of the room. It was covered with hooks and spring-clips - some of which had tools and gauges hanging from them - Vernier callipers, screw gauges, reamers, taps, dies - the whole range of hardware necessary for the production and promotion of pumps in all their stages of manufacture, from raw metal to the finely honed precision equipment leaving the factory gates en route to the Company's customers, worldwide. In the empty spaces on the board hung the tool checks of the operatives who had the items booked out to them. A simple system which could enable the tool room to trace the whereabouts of any of the tooling at any given time.

The man picked a tool check from a peg on the board and handed it to Andy.

'It's out - I think it's Baldock.' the man said.

'Ta.' Andy said, taking the brass disc and walked around to the "clocking in" machine fixed on the outside of the tool room wall. The "clocking in" cards were placed in neat rows, one beneath the other. The names of the card holders were written at the top of the stiff brown paper. Andy glanced down the rows, his eyes eventually alighting on the card which read: **R Baldock - Works Number 911**. He looked at the number on the tool check and it tallied. He walked back to the window of the tool room and held the check up to the man, 'Yep, 911 - Baldock - do you know where he is?' Andy asked.

'Ralph Baldock? - vertical drillers - centre aisle.' The man pointed over to the middle of the machine shop. 'Third one from the end on the left - it wasn't a big job - he should've finished with it by now.'

'Thanks.' Andy said, walking off in the direction he had been given.

'Bring me your check back.' the tool man said.

'Sure.' Andy said, tossing check number 911 in the air as he walked down the centre aisle.

'Look at this ponce!' said vertical driller number 911. 'I hate the bastard - him and his mates!' Baldock spat the words out to his companion, catching sight of

Andy as he walked between the rows of drills. 'They strut around as if they own the fucking town - bleedin' Mods!'
'He's on the checking slab in The Mad House.' Baldock's companion remarked.

Andy arrived at the work area of the machine and stopped near a large drum of machine oil. Baldock and his companion ceased their conversation and turned to Andy. They stared coldly, unspeaking - Andy sensed an atmosphere. He'd picked up the same vibes before in other parts of the factory over the last month or so, something then he was unable to put his finger on; he knew what was going down here - there was ice in Baldock's eyes; ice on a hot August afternoon. The Amalgamated Engineering Union had decreed that the factory be a "Closed Shop" - bigotry and prejudice decreed that some of its members had closed minds.
''you Ralph Baldock?' Andy addressed the driller.
'Mr. Baldock to you - checker.'
'Have you got the ½" Whit screw gauge?' Andy ignored the threat in Baldock's voice, but was already feeling uneasy.
'I might have ....' said Baldock turning to his companion, 'and then again I might not have.'
'Tool room say it's out on your check.' Andy said, holding up the brass disc with number 911 stamped on it.
''shouldn't believe all the tool room tell you, checker.' Baldock's refrain convinced Andy he should be out of there.
'Oh forget it.' Andy said, turning away. He didn't need this. Not today. Not today.
'Hey checker!' Baldock said, picking up the screw gauge from the flat bed of his drill, 'Catch!' and as Andy turned back to the words he hurled the heavy steel gauge directly at Andy's head. Somehow Andy managed to wrap his hands around it. The sharp die cast thread cut Andy's index finger as his palms closed around the missile. Baldock and his companion sniggered at the results of the jape.

Andy sucked his finger and shook it to relieve the pain and walking a couple of steps back to the drum of machine oil, dropped Baldock's tool check into the oil through the nozzle hole. It floated gently through the thick viscous liquid and settled on the bottom of the drum beneath 50 gallons of oil.

Baldock lunged past his companion in pursuit. He had oil on his overalls and blood (Andy's blood) in his eyes.

Education is a powerful and worthwhile facility. In those few milli-seconds Andy drew on his - on all the tales of bravery and deeds heroic, of valour in the face of insuperable odds - The Alamo, The Light Brigade, The Heroes of Thermopylae - weighed it all up instantly ... and then ran! - out of the shop, clutching the Whitworth screw gauge.

'Hey! I need your check for my board!' the man in the tool room shouted as Andy flashed passed the window.

*

Like Don, Milt's Tuesday morning was to be dominated by thoughts of sex - but Milt's pre-occupation was a reflection on his and Sharon's recent history and nature's pay back for the pleasure thereof: and like Don, Milt, contemplating the full canvas which Sharon had sketched out for him before disappearing on this blue Tuesday, couldn't face the thought of work. He was owed a couple of days from one of his last jobs, when he had worked all through three nights, re-decorating a restaurant (with little or no disruption to its trade) - and he decided to call in one of those days. In any case the firm he worked for was slack at the moment; they always were straight after the factories' holiday weeks. No one in the town seemed to have any money at the end of August or early September. He had been glad when his mother left the shed and returned to her chores inside the house, glad that Sharon had left him and gone to work. The morning with all its weekday routine seemed to purr in contentment: the faint sound of an express train in the distance, clattering through the town, on its way northbound to Edinburgh, the drone of the early morning traffic, the reassuring voice of Jack De Manio on his early morning "Today" programme, the refined jollity of the Light Programme, drifting out of the neighbours' houses and the soft plaint of the distant factory hooters all blended together in his head - heard and unheeded - but for Milt it was a routine of sham, thinly disguising a conspiracy of inevitability.

He went out of the shed and looked at the GS, resting on its stand near the door. He walked over to it, unfastened the crash hat from the rack and tossed it violently up the garden. It landed at the foot of his dad's compost heap, embedded in the decaying melange of rotting leaf, grass cuttings, tea leaves and ash.

He sat on the seat of the scooter and leaned back into the rest. Like most of the kids in the mid-60s he had never been one to look back on his life. He lived for the day, in a white heat stupor - there would be time enough for recollections. There was more than just a grain of truth in the assertion that if you could remember your good times then, in fact, you had never had any. On this day he was compelled to reflect on his future. The sun, climbing slowly and deliberately, delivering its heat, was engaged in its usual trickery of distortion and displacement. He stayed there for what seemed like hours but was, in reality, no more than a quarter of an hour: and then he opened his eyes. He got up from the seat of the scooter and started up the engine of the Vespa, with his sleeping bag still strapped to the front rack, he rode off slowly, negotiating the garden path and the back pathway to the row of houses. He turned into the covered passageway like he had done a hundred (nay, a thousand) times before and for the first time one of his wing mirrors clipped the brickwork.

His left foot went to the floor and with it a part of the 60s hit the ground.

*

He rode around the two Shires which came together at Newark and its environs, searching out the by-roads, bridle paths and back lanes. The fields he skirted around were brimming with golden swatches of spring sown wheat, oats and barley, ready for the harvest and sweating under the weight of early planted rape, which had long since swapped its bright yellow flowering blossoms for billions of seed pods, heavy with oil, which awaited the Swaffers and their ruthless art of the reaper.

The miles he covered in the morning took in the gentle hills of Bathley, Muskham, Cotham and Staunton, the flat stretches of Long Bennington and its fen, through Westborough to Norton Disney. He just had to keep moving. If he stopped he feared he might explode: it was in those terms that, for Milt, the 60s were defined.

His ride back from Carlton-Le-Moorland through Stapleford Woods had an eerie, surreal feel about it. He was alone in the lane as he rode through the two miles of densely planted forest. The twenty foot high Rhododendron bushes, which fringed both sides of the narrow road for its whole length, produced a tunnel of dense green foliage. The same bushes two months earlier had been aflame with their multi-coloured blossoms of mid-summer: now the dead heads of the flowers hung, dry and brittle, from the extremities of the branches. All passion spent.

Passing through the woods he felt he was riding in the groove of a record, with the sound of his engine bouncing and reverberating off the leaves, trees and the asphalt melting beneath his wheels - he heard the sound of his bike coming from behind and in front of him, it came from either side of him, above and below him.

He interrupted his ride eventually and, by mid-afternoon, he was parked at the Wensor Bridge which spanned the river Devon just east of Shelton village. His dad used to take him there on bike rides, when he was a kid, to see the daffodils which grew on the verges of the village. He sat with his back against the side panels of his bike, his legs stretched out on the grass. He looked across the fen land in front of him towards Sibthorpe and noticed a rising cloud of dust in the corner of a field, as the cutters of a combine took their first bites into the swollen ears of wheat.

Harvest had begun.

All manner of thoughts had raged in his head during the morning - of Sharon.

(No, the prat's getting married - selling his bike)

Of their lovemaking.

(I mean, fancy having to sell your push bike to get shacked up)

Of their baby.

(I wouldn't sell my GS for anybody!)

As the combine harvester and its trailing cloud of dust and chaff slowly approached him, he got up, removed his socks and desert boots and climbed the fence which ran along side the Devon. Down the shallow bank he slid, slipping quietly into the river at the point where, when he was nine, he had swam with his dad. Now the river only came up to his thighs and he started to walk - alienated, in the middle of the Devon, northwards under the bridge, in the direction of its junction with the Trent.

After a while the combined effects of the splashes, as he walked along the river bed and the natural capillary action of the water soaked into his Levis up to the waist band and started to wet the bottom of his T shirt. As the river widened and deepened in its meandering away from its source he was eventually up to his waist in the gentle swell of the stream and was obliged to continue the journey by swimming.

Slowly and methodically his breast stroke took him a couple of miles from the Wensor before he turned and made his way back. He dragged himself back up the bank, over the railings of the bridge and to his bike, which shone like mercury in the sunshine. He stretched out beside the scooter on the grass and watched the steam rise slowly from his sodden clothes as they started to dry on him in the fierce sun: he was tired in limb, but with his head now as crystal clear as the water he had swam through.

*

As Milt had swam, Andy had sweated. His hands and wrists were aching from the constant screwing and unscrewing of the gauge on the first few hundred of the nuts he had to check. The incident with Baldock was still in his mind as he tidied up the slab at the end of the day. He hated atmospheres, antagonism and aggravation - always had. (At school he had only ever got into one fight and that was one too many; his peers had pushed him into it, on what they had called a matter of honour and which he had regarded as a foolish and futile point of principle: it could all have been sorted by talking, but his form mates wanted the spectacle of confrontation. He had felt so confined and claustrophobic, closeted in the makeshift ring formed by a couple of hundred pressing school kids, all baying for blood - whose, it didn't matter. Andy had punched, kicked and gouged .... and lost.)

He picked up his suit from his locker and left Machine Shop "A", still wearing his overalls, making his way in the swarm of people eager, like him, to get out of the factory and cool off in the evening breeze which had started to blow. As he passed through the works' gates on foot, having declined the offer of a lift from one of his work mates on the back of a BSA Bantam, a Ford Prefect car passed close to him and he felt the slap of a hand across the back of his head and flinched as Ralph Baldock withdrew his hand and shouted abuse at him from the front window of the car: if he had need of any further reason, he was now full to the brim with the resolve to leave this dark satanic mill (and those who fuelled it) to their own devices.

He forsook his usual way home and turned left at the end of the factory service road and with his suit slung over one shoulder and sleeping bag under the other arm, walked down the lane towards the housing estate where Don lived.

He rounded the corner of Don's road and walked towards the end of the cul-de-sac. In the corner of the large sweep of tarmac, which served as a turn-around point for the half dozen end houses, stood Don's Lambretta, now shiny and glistening as a result of Don's earlier attention. He stopped briefly, admiring the machine and brushed the fur covering on the back rest which had provided him with more than mere physical support over the past couple of years. There was little sound of life, from either Don's house or any of the others in the dead end street, as he walked up the path.

He went round to the back of the house and knocked, leaning with his back against the wall as he waited for an answer to his rapping on the door. He felt like a vagrant, a vagabond and managed a smile at his visceral connection with "Baby Blue". He looked over the back gardens of the houses of this and the road beyond and could just see the black besmirched tops of the factory's extraction chimneys, breaking through the roofs of the workshops, in clear silhouette against the blue of the sky; like a minaret, hammered out of gold leaf, or a lofty spire of finely dressed stone, the chimneys dominated this part of the town - but with all the inelegance of gigantic sticks of charcoal. He could hardly bear to look at them and turned back to the door, which still remained closed to his knocking. He banged again, this time louder and shortly it was opened by Don, dressed only in his underpants, hair dishevelled: behind him was Maggie, in the same state of attire, but minus her knickers. She stood behind Don, arms around his waist and pulling tightly, squeezed a nipple under Don's armpit into the line of Andy's gaze.

'You look like a piece of crap!' Don said, eyeing Andy up and down. Maggie freed her hands and waved one at Andy, smiling broadly, but saying nothing.

'I feel like it,' Andy said wearily, 'that place's killing me.'

'Well, I've told you....' Don said, his words tailing off as Maggie slowly slid her hand down into the back of his pants.

''thought you might wanna go over to Grantham tonight.' Andy said, 'I've just got to press my suit up....'

''Can't,' Don said, 'I'm having a night in - washing my hair....' he said, as

Maggie's other arm made its way slowly down the front of his pants. She smiled. Don smiled. Andy smiled.
'OK.' Andy said, moving off. ''see you tomorrow, yeah?' Don stopped him, offering the keys to the steering column lock of the Lambretta. 'You go, take the bike - it's got a full tank of petrol.'

Andy hesitated. 'Is it insured for me?'
'Stuff the insurance - if you want it, take it - don't hang about.'
'OK.' Andy said, taking the keys, 'thanks.'
'And don't lose it!' Don said, smiled and closed the door.

Sitting on a step of a house in the next road, Ralph Baldock watched the Lambretta turn the corner of Don's cul-de-sac as Andy accelerated past him. He took a deep drag on the cigarette he was smoking and blew out the smoke with a force that might have been strong enough to knock Andy off the bike.

***

HERE COMES THE NIGHT

In the couple of weeks that followed the Bank Holiday Milt became something of a recluse. Neither Don nor Andy saw much of him and although they had called round for him on numerous occasions they'd either found him out, or just going out. There was nothing untoward in this pattern of Milt's life - they'd just put it down to him being madly in love - this state of affairs manifested itself, every few months when Milt closeted himself away with his love of the moment, with an almost total exclusion of Don and Andy. This never bothered them; indeed they came to positively relish these occasional duets; it was easier to pick up girls you were only "two up" and out on the loose and the pithy words of the proverb which pronounced that "Two's company, three's a crowd" took on a meaning of significant hedonistic proportions when they recalled some of their amazing experiences and exploits while hunting in a pack of two.

(The last time the trio had been temporarily reduced by a third was earlier in the year - again, straight after a long weekend - that of the Spring Bank Holiday. Milt had latched on to a girl from Sheffield at the Mojo Club on the Saturday night before they had ridden through the night to the east coast. She was the double of Marianne Faithfull, sophisticated, mysterious and, as he had later expounded, "as hot as Lincolnshire tarmac and the tailpipe of his GS after a two hour ride".

That Bank Holiday weekend was a total wipe-out for Milt - his head throughout the whole three days was back in Sheffield, stuffed with thoughts of her, instead of its usual filling of Amphetamine and other equally infusive narcotic cocktails.

In the three or four weeks that followed, he'd left Don and Andy to their own pursuits and had mixed some fairly erratic shift working with some equally erotic sheet work in this girl's flat in Tinsley. He had frequently ridden the forty odd miles to South Yorkshire after work, returning home in the early hours of the morning or sometimes riding straight to work, kept awake on a diet of pills, adrenaline and promises. On his journeys back from Sheffield he'd crouched low over the fly screen of the GS, tucking his knees well inside the front boards, his body offering as little resistance to the wind as it had to the far-out sex in which they had indulged in the rooms of the apartment, which looked out over the bright lights and flaming chimney stacks of a city, full of tales of stainless steel and Stringfellow's Soldiers.)

Don and Andy had thus carried on with the familiar pattern of their days without Milt. Their time was divided up between the usual brimming segments of their lives as Mods - drinking and dancing, posing and polishing - all the meticulous attention to the minutiae of style and mechanical adjustment. This was underwritten by the wages of their day jobs; as Andy had come to realise, in the couple of weeks since the Bank Holiday, his chosen career was particularly evil - but a necessary one for all that. His meagre subsistence wages were, to a large extent, supplemented by Don's healthier pay packets - but they both accepted the need for a regular income to fund their life out in the streets and in the dance halls and clubs.

The Mod ethic was thus nurtured and cherished silently and secretly in hundreds of thousands of private means and occupations - factory hands, shop assistants, floor walkers, machine operators, bank tellers, refuse collectors and insurance clerks were sucked into its vortex - all united in diversity, yet totally apolitical in stance and with no obvious leaders. The ethic transcended social barriers, caring nothing for whence you came or where you were bound, but only ***how*** you travelled.

Don's work was hard and dirty, but was free of the complications which were tossed in Andy's path at the factory, in pursuit of his pathetic apprentice wages. His French teacher, a vehement traditionalist and hater of Andy's 4th year crew cut, had said that if all else failed he could always get a job as a lavatory brush - Andy was already regretting not having taken this advice, considering all the shit lumped on him in his job. He was beginning to think there wasn't a pay packet big enough to compensate for all the crap he was being forced to eat in his capacity as a checker of other people's work.

The six thousand Whitworth nuts had now been thoroughly gone through and he'd been obliged to reject over a third of them on account of the tapping being too deep on the screw threads - the machine operator concerned had blamed Andy, his machine, the tool room, the tool and the fact that Forest had lost at home three times on the trot - none of which were sufficient reasons to absolve himself from responsibility for producing an expensive pile of scrap.

The charge hand ultimately responsible for the lad's work had given Andy more grief than a cross threaded spark plug in an alloy cylinder head - trying all manner of cajoling and persuasion in an attempt to reverse Andy's decision.

If he'd tried bribery he might well have succeeded.

There followed a job from over at the main Machine Shop Number "1" for Andy to check - the checkers there were stacked out with work and this particular job was a special contract for the Admiralty - half a dozen centrifugal pumps, constructed out of some special new cadmium steel, which was already three weeks behind its scheduled completion date. It was Andy's job to check the flanges on the casings and impeller covers.

'Here you go Andy,' Harry said to him as he signed for the job, 'your chance to make a name for yourself - check the stud tappings and the locating holes on the casings carefully - apparently they're crucial. '

Andy nodded and watched in silence as the banksman gave directions to the overhead crane operator. The pulley on the crane's jib creaked and heaved under the weight of the chains as it lowered the pallets containing the shiny steel pumps to the floor in front of Andy. Harry passed Andy the drawing for the job and he spread it over the checking slab, studied and became au fait with it before slowly checking the dimensions and positioning of each of the machined operations on the pump casings against the measurements on the drawings.

Twenty minutes into the job and he was scratching his head - he checked the facings on the flanges with his straight edge and both were engineered to perfection. The centres of the studs and the stud holes in the base and impeller cover were also spot on. He checked the drawing again and once more ran his ruler over the diameters of the drill holes around both casings and covers - that was where the problem lay. Andy checked the drawing again - it clearly called for holes of 1/2" diameter - those actually drilled into the casings were 7/8".

Andy called Harry over to the slab and his boss confirmed the problem.

Harry was soon in the office and on the 'phone to his counterpart in Machine Shop Number "1". The drawing for the job was spread out on the desk.

'George? - Harry..... I've no problem, but I'd say your lot have.... that Admiralty job - well my lad's just checked it ..... you've got someone who can't read over there - why?....The studs in the casings are 7/8" - 'says 1/2" on the drawing. Exactly! - the driller?'

Harry checked the legend on the drawing, which identified everyone who'd been involved with the job from its initial casting in the foundry, through the fettling shop, to the milling room and the machining operations

'Your driller ? - Number 911. OK. - I'll get the labourer to cart them back over to you..... cheers George.'

Three hours after the offending pump casings had been returned to Machine Shop Number "1" for the inquest on why over a month's work had ended up as an expensive pile of scrap, Andy found himself on the floor, beside the checking slab, being kicked and punched by vertical driller Number 911. The onslaught had taken Andy unawares and before Harry and a couple of the nearby operatives managed to pull Ralph Baldock off Andy's prone form, he had taken a couple of heavy punches to his face (one of which had cut his eye) and several kicks in the ribs from Baldock's size nine, steel capped, work boots.

'Bastard! Bastard!' shouted Baldock, 'you Mod bastard checker!' as he was being dragged off Andy, still trying to rain blows on the one who'd rejected his work.

'You Mod Bastard - you shopped me! Fucking Mod ponce!' Baldock was still screaming his tirade of abuse as he was manhandled into the yard which ran between the two machine shops.

Andy got up and found that the whole shop had virtually ground to a standstill to watch the removal of Baldock - as a Mod, Andy was well used to being a focal point - his whole life style was based on the amount attention he could command from his peers; but he needed this scene like a hole in his pay packet. He straightened his hair and re-arranged himself. He was in an emotional state - and he hurt - Baldock had possessed a strength amplified by hatred. Harry put his hand on Andy's shoulder but Andy roughly shrugged him away. 'I was only doing my job.' Andy choked and Harry turned back, but without any answer to Andy's words. 'Only doing my job Harry - what's that got to do with being a Mod?'

Apparently it had everything to do with him being a Mod; of all the jobs in the factory that of a checker carried a stigma of mistrust and complicity. To the rank and file of the workers on the shop floor checkers were aligned with the bosses, the gaffers. In the cradle of adversarial industrial politics rocking in the mid 60s, the syndrome of "them and us", checkers (and their last words) were regarded, not as a vital link in the chain of quality control but, with some degree of suspicion, as the hirelings of management. If, like Andy, you set out to be studiously different in the way you lived then you also had a Parka full of other problems to contend with.

He spent the rest of the shift maintaining a low profile; he stayed near the slab for the duration of the mid-afternoon break, knowing that the talk over tea would be about him. (Don would have told him to assert himself - spit in the face of them all - but he wasn't Don.) He'd also refused a visit to the factory nurse, although his ribs ached from those kicks which had found their target. At the end of the break Harry called him across. 'That burk of a driller's been given his marching orders, I'm told. Apparently he's been warned times before about the standard of his work and that little ta-ta in here with you was the last straw.'
Andy said nothing in reply to the information Harry had imparted. Great, he thought, now I'm responsible for him losing his job!

*

It took a couple of days for the pain in his ribs to subside completely and the ache had been painful accompaniment to the thoughts which had engaged him since Baldock had been sacked. Andy knew that Don and Milt would have retaliated against what had happened in the run-in with Baldock, just to clean the slate, but Andy had been phased by the whole rotten mess of it all and, having resolved to get out of the job as quickly as possible, didn't wish for any more attention to be heaped on himself. Picking over how his friends would have handled the incident brought back thoughts of Milt and how he'd probably soon be back in circulation again, when either he, or the woman he was undoubtedly studying, got bored and called off the affair.

It was therefore a shock to him when, skipping through the Classified Ads section of the Nottingham Evening Post one Friday evening, he saw an advert for a scooter. The first three words were in bold type and as he read it in full, including the address and the neighbour's telephone number, amidst the other bikes on offer, it was plain to him that this was no ordinary advert - it offered Milt's scooter for sale.

He re-read the advert through three more times in the hope that his eyes were deceiving him and then he put the paper down. God, he thought what was happening? As all the reasons and possibilities for Milt's actions raced through his head the irony of the situation was lost on him - he couldn't have sold ***his*** bike if he'd wanted to - he hadn't finished paying for it yet. Why should Milt want to sell his?

*

Milt was in his back yard as Andy started out for his friend's house to find out the answer to the question. The yard was full of the cleaning gear for his bike - cloths, dusters and polishes. A bucket, containing the remains of the soapy water with which he'd washed the bike, stood near the fence which divided the yard from that of the neighbouring house. He'd rinsed the suds from the Vespa with clean water, dispensed from one of his dad's watering cans and it now stood next to the bucket. He had sponged up the water which had collected, on the running boards, trapped between the rubber topped foot rails - the rest of the clean rinsing water had run down the softly sloping surfaces of the scooter, taking with it the last remnants of the suds. This had dripped into the surface of the yard and spread laterally, creating a dark grey underlay beneath and around the bike, which seemed to underline the presence of the scooter, shining and gleaming - a pearl amongst its drab surroundings of faded concrete and the sun bleached timber of the fence. He had polished the chrome work with Solvol Autosol polish - this was something usually employed in the shining up of motor cycle brightwork - megaphone silencers, chrome manifolds, front suspension cylinders etc. but it was fantastic stuff and Milt forgave its association with the grease machines.

When the last smears of water had been leathered away with a chamois and the sun had dried off the paintwork Milt had covered its cellulose with wax polish and after the liqueous coating had metamorphosed into its semi-solid state he had set about the wax with a sheepskin buffer. With a singularity of purpose he transformed every inch of the paintwork into a curved mirror, reflecting the images of the yard and the surrounding brickwork of the house and outbuildings.

The scooter was a Vespa GS 150 model. It had started its life in Italy painted a nondescript light blue, but Milt had given it the treatment after he'd bought it - he'd had the bulbous side panels and the front mudguard chromium plated (this had cost him a small fortune but he reckoned it was worth every penny); to complement the side panels, he'd added a set of chrome front and rear crash bars - the front set traced a parallel line around the curve of the front panel and the rear ones wrapped themselves around the bottom of each of the side panels, bolted into place at the back below the rear number plate mounting and fastened at the front onto the pillion passenger's footrest, beneath the petrol tap.

The bike had a fly screen and, like Don's Lambretta, had the word NEWARK written on it in the same white script lettering. The front rack carried an array of mirrors on stalks and the light from the single head lamp built into the handlebars was supplemented by three additional spot lights fastened to a horizontal chromium bar, bolted through the front panels with each of the bolt entry holes protected by a shiny rubber grommet.

The back rack was in a caravan, somewhere in Ingoldmells.

All the remaining paintwork of the Vespa, originally finished in Piaggio's minimalist but insipid livery, had been covered with seven coats of deep metallic purple cellulose, topped by a coat of lacquer which made it shine in varying degrees of intensity, depending on the amount of sunlight on the pigments in the paint. On this day it reflected a bright, almost cobalt hue of Mediterranean intensity.

The seat had been ripped when he'd took delivery of the scooter, and it had been recovered in white PVC - (he'd wanted it done in leather, but the coach trimmer who'd performed the re-upholstery had pointed out that you could wipe PVC dry in a couple of minutes but with leather you'd have a wet backside for maybe a couple of days).

He flicked the last piece of solidified wax off the speedo cowl and ran his hands slowly over the breast like rear panels.

It would be the last time he would ever polish and cosset the machine.

Andy arrived with the newspaper folded open at the page which carried the advert for Milt's bike. Milt was clearing away his polishing materials.
'What are you selling it for?' Andy blurted out to Milt, doing away with the usual salutations at a reunion of friends. He waved the newspaper between the two of them.
'Because I need the money.' Milt said, he too dispensing with the formality which normally accompanies the renewal of an acquaintance.
'How are you gonna get around?' Andy asked, looking at Milt's GS, resplendent in all its raging glory.
'Fucking walk!' Milt said carrying an armful of his polishes and cleaning cloths back into the wash house.
Andy looked perplexed as Milt emerged clapping his hands together, removing the powdery deposits from the dusters; a small cloud of white dust rose above his palms.
'Why?' Andy asked.
' 'cos I need the money! I told you.' Milt snapped.
'Why!' Andy repeated.
'None of your fucking business.' Milt rounded on Andy but changed his tone immediately, which he meant and Andy took, as an apology.
'Sharon's pregnant....'
'Jeez.' Andy whistled through his teeth, that explained everything, including Milt's hibernation of late. He tossed the newspaper into the dustbin nearby.
'Fancy a drink?' Andy said, for want of something to say, if nothing else.
'To celebrate me selling the GS?' Milt replied drily. In those words there was an ambivalence - a mixture of rage tempered with fatalism.
'Why, 'you had anybody after it?' Andy enquired.
'A couple of time wasters,' Milt replied, 'but one of the Sutton scooter lads is definitely interested, he's coming to see it tomorrow.'
Andy's heart sank with those words.

*

They drank alone - Don had a date with Maggie and had taken her to "The Dungeon" in Nottingham - they talked about some of their good times - well those they could remember - walking home the fourteen miles from Grantham one Saturday night, unable to hitch a lift after they'd punctured a tyre without a spare - their joint appearance in court for riding home "two up" on the GS before Milt had passed his test - pissing wet through while eating beans on soggy toast in a café in Barnsley, which had slowly filled up with Greasers - yep, all the remembered good times.

Andy had never been one to crave for alcohol but that Friday night he had more than his usual pint and a half. By the end of the night Milt and he had drunk well into his pay packet. The alcohol had exposed his sentimental streak.

'It's all gonna fold up.' Andy sighed.

'What is?' Milt asked puzzled.

'I can sense it.' Andy said finishing another pint.

'What are you on about?' said Milt, beer gave him strength and unlike a lot of people, actually cleared his head.

'Us - Mods.' Andy said, 'You're selling your bike. That's the beginning of the end.' He continued, 'It's gonna be just like school. You're there for five years - find some great mates, then the bell rings for the last time on your last day and you walk out of the gates and nobody sees anybody ever again.....' He had forgotten how, when at school, he couldn't wait to leave it; but then, like a lot of people, he'd never known what he'd had until it was gone.

'Andy,' Milt said, after listening patiently to Andy's self-pitying soliloquy, 'stop being so bloody maudlin' - you know what the gig is. I've got Sharon pregnant and I need some money. So the GS has to go.' He sounded resigned to the loss of the Vespa.

'Are you getting married?' Andy asked.

'I'm getting rid.' Milt said in reply.

'Rid?' Andy queried.

'Sharon's gonna have an abortion.' Milt lowered his voice.

'God.' Andy said in a tone equally as soft.

'So I need the money, right.'

'Have you asked Don?' Andy asked.

'It's not Don's problem,' Milt answered coolly, 'besides, he's too busy subsidising you - you bugger.' Milt beamed across at his friend. There was no malice inferred towards him, but Andy felt it - and felt dreadful, in contemplation of the problem which they were, in a sense, both responsible for. If Andy had more disposable income they wouldn't be contemplating the sale of Milt's GS. There followed a temporary silence between them - the first one of the evening: Andy broke it.
'So if you had some money then you wouldn't have to sell the GS?'
'You're a bright one Andrew.' Milt said sarcastically, 'Right in one!'
Another silence followed as they finished their drinks and left the pub. They walked, without speaking, across the cobbled market place until their respective paths home parted.
'Don't sell the GS.' Andy said as they were about to take their separate ways home. 'I'll get the money - somehow.'
'Andy,' Milt replied, 'when have you ever got two spare ha'pennies to rub to gether?'

*

Andy emerged from Will's house with twenty five pounds in his pocket and poverty in his soul.

*

'How much d'you say?' the Mod from Sutton in Ashfield said, 'Seventy five?'
'Eighty.' Milt said as he watched the youth pace around the gleaming Vespa, like a lion ready to kill. The prospective purchaser sat on the seat of the scooter, turned the handlebars and crouched low over the fly screen. Milt had already removed the white lettering which had spelt NEWARK.
'Why are you selling it?' the youth asked.
'There's nothing wrong with it - if that's what you're thinking.' Milt replied coldly. The lad from Sutton dismounted, walked away a couple of paces and turned to view it from a different angle.
'Well do you want it?' Milt asked again impatiently. How he'd come this far in the painful process of the sale was nothing short of a minor miracle and now he wanted the transaction completed quickly.

'Yep - I want it,' the Sutton boy confirmed, 'might change the colour though - get it resprayed.'
' 's been resprayed.' Milt sounded annoyed.
'It's not my colour - but I want it.' The youth remounted the bike and patted the rear seat. 'It hasn't got a back rack?' he queried.
'It's a long story.' Milt sighed.

The lad made no further enquiry and pulled out his wallet from the breast pocket of his Parka. He started to count eighty pounds in notes from within it - a fiver at a time. As he was on the fifteenth note Milt piped up, 'Seventy five if you keep it the same colour.'
The Mod looked up from his wallet. 'You what?'
'You can have it for seventy five....' Milt repeated, 'if you don't get it resprayed.'
'Why?' the youth looked puzzled.
'I'm sentimental.' Milt said. 'Leave it as it is.'
'I could take it for seventy five and still get it resprayed - you might never know.' the Mod from Sutton in Ashfield smiled.
'You could - but you won't.' Milt said to the youth.
'O.K. - done - 'got the log book?'

In those terms the sale of one Vespa GS150 motor scooter was struck.
The Sutton scooter lad took the log book and satisfied himself with the details therein.
'Are you gonna ride it away?' Milt asked, anxious now to conclude the deal. 'It's taxed 'til October.'
'I've got no insurance on it,' the Mod shook his head.
Milt nipped into his front door and came out with an envelope. He handed it to the youth - 'Here's the insurance policy and my licence - if the law stops you then you're Peter Milton - you can send them back to me in the post, when you get it insured properly in your name. The address is on the policy.'
'O.K.' the youth confirmed and put the documents in his Parka pocket.

Milt's Vespa was now part of the famous Sutton scooter lads' fleet. The proud new owner of the bike switched on the petrol at the tap and thrust his foot downwards, flooring the kick start. It sprang back up from the recoil in the magneto. Exactly the right amount of petrol gushed into the carburettor, measured meticulously by the needle in its float chamber; air was forced through the filter and rushed towards the petrol; this mixture was sucked into the cylinder head via the inlet valve, which then closed. The trapped mixture was compressed and exploded by a spark from the plug's electrode; the exhaust valve opened and the spent mixture was pumped out of the manifold and expelled through the bike's exhaust system into the street. Four thousand times per minute the engine's two-stroke operation was repeated as the bike was revved. The clutch was disengaged, first gear selected on the handlebar's twist grip and the lever released slowly, carefully. The power of the piston was transferred to the rear wheel by the bike's transmission and thus, with Milt, Andy saw the Vespa move off in the direction of Sutton in Ashfield as he rounded the corner of the street - with twenty five pounds burning a hole in his pocket.

'What have you done?!' Andy cried, as he arrived at Milt's house, breathless from sprinting in the direction of the disappearing Vespa.

'What's it look like?' Milt replied drily.

'I've got the money Milt,' Andy was near to tears, 'twenty five - for you and Sharon - to get it all sorted out.' Andy offered Milt the money. Milt turned away.

'Thanks Andy, thanks alot, but it's not enough anyway, so you needn't have bothered....' He started to walk towards the covered passageway to the back of his house.

'I've sold my bike.'

'Milt, I've just sold my backside.....'

As Milt turned around he could see Andy had started to cry. His head was bowed low but he could see the tears running down his cheeks. He turned back to Andy, whose hand, stuffed with the five pound notes, hung loosely by his side. Milt was speechless. What could he say? What words were there?

***

AS TEARS GO BY

Neither Andy nor Milt wanted each other's company after the Mod from Sutton had ridden off on Milt's bike. Milt, who thought he'd come to terms with its loss - hadn't, and Andy well....

He walked back towards home past Will's house and carried on at the top of the street and up the lane, passing his old junior school, which once had been of such a new and revolutionary design and construction, built nine years ago in the year he had started juniors, but now looked tatty and incredibly old fashioned.

He walked over the first railway bridge, which spanned the branch line, running from the shunting yards in Newark Station and the old loco sheds. It was here in his train spotting days where he'd copped the whole of the 9F class, including "Evening Star".

He moved along onto the next bridge over the main line, not thirty yards away. It was on this bridge that Andy and his friends would, for dares, walk across the parapet, (even when there was ice on it in winter), as steam trains clattered beneath, enshrouding them in a white cloud of billowing steam, removing all visibility as they walked confidently across it. He could still remember the sight of a line of his friends on top of the bridge emerging, one by one, like ghosts, from the white fog of steam from the engine's funnels - as if he'd led them through some secret passageway from Hades (which was, in effect, where he was now coming from).

The memories from those days chilled him as he crossed the bridge. The expanse of grass, from the bridge down to the mock-Tudor house at the head of the dell in the opposite corner, stretched in front of him. There were two kids playing on the concrete cricket strip in the middle of the field, the only piece of recreational facility left since the swings, roundabout and slide had been taken away.

He had, on the face of it, no apparent reason for walking to this particular place, but in reality it was a journey on which he was spurred by his subconscious, mapped by the landmarks of his pre-adolescent days - a journey harking back to an age of innocence. An age of steam trains and all day cricket matches in rainless summer holidays.

He passed the spiked railings which fenced off the entrance to the waterworks and its gate, passed the gingerbread cottage, framed with roses and then, as the metal surface of the road petered out into rutted clay, baked hard by the sun, he stopped at the entrance to the field on the left. It was covered in Buttercups which sprayed their yellow covering right up to the borders of Dalton's Wood, at the foot of the slope towards Beacon Hill. There were a couple of dozen horse chestnuts in the far corner of this field. One clump was called the Seven Sisters by all the kids in the neighbourhood.

He couldn't believe how small the field looked on this day - he had always thought of it as immense, when, in the company of his friends from junior school, they had collected its conkers. But close by the gate stood the landmark of this locality; the enormity of the tree he stood looking at could not be distorted by time. It was immense - a huge Horse Chestnut, which grew twenty yards from the gate at the edge of the field but whose branches spread beyond the Hawthorn hedge, providing a huge canopy over the lane.

The base of its trunk was over thirty feet in circumference and its first stout, low branches spread laterally for what seemed miles - an open invitation to be climbed. This tree seemed ageless; it could have been five hundred or a thousand years old, for all Andy and his early school friends knew.

They called it King Kong. After all those years he remembered the easiest way up the tree, as he climbed it on this black Friday. It must have been four or five years since he'd last made his way skywards here, by way of its branches and as he climbed he passed several sets of his initials, still clearly visible, carved in the bark, marking the height up the tree he'd managed to reach over the years he'd scaled it.

On this day he climbed past the last of his carved initials and was into new territory. He slowly negotiated his way towards the top of the tree, passing the spot from which the Bartlett lad had fallen but who had picked himself up with nothing more than a few bruises on body and pride, the branches having broken the fall.

The wind rustled the leaves of this giant of a tree, laden with its fruit concealed within the light green husks, as he climbed no more but sat in the fork of a branch near the top of the Horse Chestnut. He'd never climbed so high - nor felt so low.

For how long he stayed there he wasn't sure; this was not a day of which he wished to be reminded in any permanent way. Today there were to be no initials carved into the bark as a record of where he'd been. No pointer to how high he had climbed - or how low he'd sank.

*

On arriving back at his house he went straight to the wash house and lifted the large zinc bath tub from its hook on the wall. He dragged it across the yard and into the back room of the house; he pushed the dining table back to make room for the grey metal tub in front of the fire grate. His mother, on hearing the noise he was making, came into the back kitchen and remarked that he never usually had a bath this particular day. He was fairly uncommunicative, muttering something under his breath, and his mother left him, returning to the front room - she had learned, over the years, never to discourage children from bathing.

He took the huge galvanised pan, which the household used for heating bath water, from beneath the sink and filled it from the kitchen tap. After he'd placed it on the stove and lit the gas he then flicked on the switch of the electric water geyser, whose spout hung over the sink. He stood in silence, waiting for both to heat the water within.

He could, if he'd wanted, have gone to the slipper baths in the town's covered market and have had as much hot water that the nine pence admission would purchase - but this was to be a ritual bathing, a symbolic cleansing, an attempt at renovation after the prostitution of himself - and not some quick and convenient "wash and brush up". Whether or not it would serve any real or tangible purpose he cared not, but felt it was something that had to be done.

When the water was boiling on the gas stove he tipped it into the bath and repeated the procedure and after a couple more full pans, hot from the geyser, went into the bath, he topped it up almost to the rim from the hot tap, still luke warm from the morning's use of the immersion heater: the water was hot to his skin as he slipped into the tub, but he gritted his teeth and immersed himself.

He needed to take some pain in his penance.

As he lay in the bath, in a pathetic attempt to soak away the stain on his life, he lowered his head into the suds, as if the removal of himself from the world above the water line would somehow erase the harm he had done to himself.

As if.

He emerged, gasping for air and noticed it had started to rain. As a young child he had, for what seemed now a million times, lain on his bed after a summer rain storm, waiting for the signs, in the drying out of the tiles on the wash house roof, that rain had stopped. In those blue, remembered days the sure sign of the sun was the slow change in colour, from dark to light, of the grey slates, steaming in the heat.

Now he was asking himself, would it ever stop raining?

Never more;
Miranda,
Never more.
Only the high peaks of hoar:
And Aragon a torrent at the door.
No sound
In the walls of the Halls where falls
The tread
Of the feet of the dead to the ground.
No sound:
Only the boom
Of the far Waterfall like Doom.

He scrubbed at himself, using copious amounts of soap and the ferocity with which he wielded the scrubbing brush broke the skin in a couple of places on the backs and palms of his hands. The soap stung as it entered the abrasions.

At the end of his bath he felt a little better, but not that radically altered. The ritual was to be continued in the decanting of the now grey sudsy water from the bath down the outside drain: with this process complete he dragged the bath back across the yard to the wash house and hoisted it back on to its hook. He was wearing only his jeans - his shoes, socks and shirt were in the house, draped over the chair where he'd placed them before his bath.

As he turned back, after closing the door of the wash house, he saw his father across the yard, standing in the back door. In his hand his father held the twenty five pounds from Andy's pocket.

'Where'd you get this from?' his father addressed him sternly. 'It fell out of your shirt pocket when your mother came through.'

Andy stopped and looked at his dad, unable to offer any explanation. The rain started to drip down his neck - he was becoming as wet as he had been whilst in the bath.

'Well - where'd you get it!?' his father snapped.

'Somebody owed me it.' Andy said softly.

'When've you had twenty five pounds to lend anybody Andrew?' his father asked.

'It was from a deal I did.' Andy shifted his weight nervously from one foot to another.

'You better make up your mind,' his father said, 'or make up another story.'

'I didn't steal it, if that's what you're thinking.' Andy retorted.

'Well, what do you want me to think Andrew? - when sticking out of your son's pocket is more money than he earns in a month eh?'

'Look dad I didn't steal it.'

'Is it drugs then?' his father advanced a couple of paces from the shelter of the doorway, 'Because if it is....'

'It's not drugs and I didn't steal it.' Andy was emphatic. His father looked on, unsmiling.

'I did a favour for it.' Andy said quietly, lowering his eyes away from his father's gaze.

'Who for?'
'For Milt - I did a favour for Milt.'
'Well it stinks to me,' his dad said, returning to the kitchen door. He turned around, 'If you bring trouble here Andrew....'

Andy interrupted him, 'Dad, let's just say I have it - and I didn't steal it - there won't be any trouble....'
He moved a couple of paces towards his father. 'Can I have it please?' He stretched out a hand towards his father and closed his wet palm around the notes and stood in the rain, watching his father disappear inside the house.

*

Andy was sitting on the side of the Trent, looking across at the Castle opposite. The concrete on which he was seated was still wet from the rain and the seat of his jeans was damp. His feet dangled over the edge of the girder reinforced bank, which was usually full of pleasure boats, moored up to the heavy iron stantions set into the concrete cappings which formed this section of the water way. The mooring stretched from the bridge up to the Town Lock; a single cabin cruiser, bobbing gently in the river's stream, was anchored close to the Lock.

He had skimmed stones from the opposite bank to where he now sat. He could get them all the way across.

He contemplated the Castle. It was a part of the psyche of anyone who lived in Newark, and it still filled him with awe every time he saw it. It rose from the banks of the river, where once the Fosse Way had crossed The Great North Road - a by-pass now took the through traffic around and away from its grey buildings, but its presence was heavy, brooding - menacing but romantic.

King John died in it. Cromwell bombarded it with shot fired from a cannon named "Sweet Lips", after a prostitute from Hull.

King : Barons. Cromwell : Charles I.
Roundheads : Cavaliers. Cowboys : Indians.
Mods : Rockers. Rich : Poor.
Them : Us. Winners : Losers.
Haves : Havenots.

It was all tied up in the relationship of opposites.

Forces, the results of interactions of two bodies, always appear in pairs. In each pair the forces are equal in magnitude and opposite in direction.

Newton's Laws of Motion (Law 3)

Why at this moment in his life, was he thinking about grammar school Physics?

He pulled the twenty five pounds from his back pocket and rustled the paper in his hand. As far as he could remember he had only touched a five pound note once - a few years back when, one week, his dad had let him help divide up his wage packet between the various weekly expenses. Even when he bought his scooter the transaction had been cashless HP, clinical in its legal formalities. His suit had been paid for in dribs and drabs.

The money rustled in his palm for the last time before Andy let it drop from his hand. There was no savouring the moment. Let it go. Let it go. It seemed like decades as it floated down to the waters of the river. He hoped the current of the Trent would take it right out through the Humber Estuary, into the North Sea; out of sight (out of mind?).

If he'd been paid by Will with one of the silver "Siege Pieces", minted in the 1640's, during the town's two Civil War sieges, the payment (if it wasn't to help Milt) would still have ended up in the Trent.

When he raised his eyes from the water and looked across to the ground sloping away from beneath the Castle's buttresses he noticed that the grassy bank was the exact colour of his suit.

As the notes floated gently away from Andy, towards the bridge, a part of the 60s was washed away.

***

CONCRETE AND CLAY

The bus journey to Nottingham was made in silence. Sharon sat upright in the seat, both hands tightly clasped around the stainless steel grip bar which ran along the back of the seat in front.

Milt had the window seat and sat staring out at the countryside rolling past his eyes. They had missed the Nottingham "Direct" bus and had taken the one which went through the villages. The beauty of the scenery on the meandering route through some of Nottinghamshire's most picturesque villages was totally lost on both of them. They were shook and jolted in their seats while the bus negotiated the narrow roads and tight bends as it plied between the villages which lay to the east of the Fosse.

Some fields were laden with golden swathes of spring sown crops, awaiting harvest, swaying at the whim of the breeze. Golden. Ripe. Swollen.

Occasionally Sharon rested her hand on her stomach. It would, she thought, be the closest she would ever get to touching the child inside her. Her sideways glances made no eye contact with Milt, whose head rested on the side of the glass, in an attempt to cool his head in the oppressive heat of the bus.

Eventually, the bus regained the Fosse and crossed over the road to the villages which nestled on its western flank. The last part of the journey was made on the road which ran from RAF Newton to Radcliffe on Trent - the Low Road. Milt loved it. It was a rider's road - narrow, windy - and dangerous.

The windsock at the back of RAF Newton flapped gently as the bus passed it. The land falling away from the road to the right was the southern side of the Trent's wide valley. Shelford village snuggled on the river's edge, at the foot of the hill and the Trent snaked its way under Gunthorpe Bridge to Newark, in the distance.

The last time Milt had travelled this way had been on the GS in a full throttled, tyre squealing run through this four mile chicane of a road. On the numerous occasions he had travelled it, alone or racing Don and Andy, the scenery never figured in the equation of getting from A to B in the shortest possible time - then his eyes were only on the grey tarmac and the white line which traced its twisty route.

Today was different. Although he showed no interest, he was compelled to look - look at how perfect the valley of the Trent was - how each turn in the road opened up a new idyllic vista of the Shire, as it clung to the contours of the valley. Every tree, every interlocking pantile, every hedge, every field, all fitting so neatly into the patchwork jig-saw of England in this high summer time; this quiet ideal made the journey almost unbearable. He was glad when the bus rumbled into the station on Huntingdon Street and they slipped quietly and anonymously into the city.

*

He pulled the money fron his wallet and handed it to Sharon. The cash from the sale of his scooter had been supplemented by both himself and Sharon and now amounted to a little over a hundred pounds.
'D'you think it'll be alright Milt?' she said, 'Maggie Risley was bad for weeks afterwards.'
Milt shrugged, unable to communicate, as they stood outside the building. Sharon was numbed by the dead weight of her circumstances and started to cry.
'I wish I had my mum with me.' she sobbed.
'You haven't told your Ma have you?' Milt sounded anxious.
'No, but I still wish she was here.' she said searching for a handkerchief in her handbag. Milt pulled his from his pocket and turned towards her. She still fumbled inside her bag, unaware of Milt hovering over her uneasily. He backed off a few paces, held back, unable to offer her the support she needed.

(Would the question in Milt's life ever be answered, as to how he came to form an emotional attachment to the GS, which was, in essence, a lump of steel and chrome, while maintaining such detatchment from another machine - soft but more complex and demanding - Sharon?)

'It'll be alright.' He tried his best.
'It's alright for you to say that.' Sharon snapped, 'You don't have to go through with it.'
'What do you want me to say Sharon? - if I could swop places with you I would.'
'Would you?'

They climbed the stairs and presented themselves to the receptionist and were shown to a private waiting area. Sharon had wiped her eyes but they still looked sore and bloodshot from the salt water.

Eventually, Sharon was summoned by a woman in a white nurses uniform. She turned to Milt as she was ushered out of the room. Neither spoke.

Milt waited - for how long he wasn't sure; the place was neat, functional, clinical - the plethora of glass and chromium plated "state of the art" furniture reminded him of the GS.

He felt oppressed by the room and went out into the street to get some fresh air. He was aimlessly kicking a discarded cigarette packet along the gutter when Sharon came out of the clinic. She was upset, distressed and aggitated. Milt stared at her. 'Sharon, what's up - what are you doing - can't they do it?'
'Milt, oh Milt, I couldn't! I can't. I wish my mum was here.'
'What d'you mean you can't!' Milt exploded, 'Christ, I've sold my GS for this!.....well, where is it then!' Milt screamed, grabbing her handbag, 'The money I got for my GS!'

Sharon grabbed hold of the handbag and they each struggled for possession of it. Milt's superior strength wrested the handbag from Sharon and he turned his back to her, shielding it from her continued attempts to take it back from him.
'C'mon where is it?' he said, delving into her purse.
'Milt - no - I'll need the money for clothes and things, for the baby - please!'

'Screw you - jeez, I didn't sell my GS for baby clothes!

*

The three of them together visited Sharon in hospital. As they approached the main reception area Andy noticed a large plastic sign to the side of the desk. It read:-

IN ORDER TO PRESERVE STERILE CONDITIONS IN THIS HOSPITAL WOULD ANY VISITORS HAVING BEEN IN CONTACT WITH PERSONS SUFFERING FROM CONTAGIOUS OR INFECTIOUS DISEASES PLEASE REPORT TO RECEPTION BEFORE PROCEEDING TO THE WARDS.

'Hang on!' said Andy, after reading the notice and veered off towards the reception, taking Don and Milt along with him.
'Excuse me.' Andy said to the woman on reception, who was busy writing. He pointed to the sign at the reception desk. 'Excuse me, but I've got a bit of a cold.'
'I'm sorry Sir. We don't have a vacant bed for you at the moment,' the woman replied, trying to present a straight face to Andy's serious tones, 'but if you'd like to come back next week I'm sure we could sort something out for you. '
'No, but the notice says....' Andy's sentence was interrupted by Don and Milt pulling him away from the now giggling receptionist.
'You prat!' said Don, 'and I thought you had an education.'

Milt was quiet, but managed to smile, as he led them to the ward to find Sharon.. Milt had brought a bouquet of flowers, Don a couple of bunches of grapes and Andy's offering was a clutch of Michaelmas Daisies.

Milt handed the bouquet to Sharon, who seemed genuinely pleased to receive her visitors - especially Milt. Don handed her the brown paper bag full of grapes, seated himself beside the bed and promptly started eating them.
'Hey, don't eat the lady's grapes!' Milt admonished, bringing a large vase full of water back to the bedside for the flowers.
'It's traditional... you always eat the patient's fruit.' Don said, pulling out a couple of seeds from the soft green flesh he'd just bitten into.

Andy handed Sharon the flowers he'd brought. There was no paper around them and as Sharon took them she brushed away the dirt which had fallen from them onto the starched white sheets she lay beneath. 'Andy, they've still got the soil on them!' she laughed, putting them on her bedside table.

'Yeah, I know,' Andy said, 'I lifted 'em from the garden of one of the Almshouses opposite.' he said, helping her brush away the last few pieces of soil, 'D'you like them?' he smiled.

They stayed around her bedside, eating her grapes and chocolates and drinking her Lucozade, idly chatting about nothing in particular, generally trying to keep her smiling. Eventually Don and Andy went off in search of the toilets.

Milt remained with Sharon. The bed was at the end of the ward and the curtains were closed around the next patient, giving Sharon a modicum of privacy. Milt moved away and stared out of the window over the park.

'I'm sorry Milt. I didn't want it like this....honestly.' Sharon spoke quietly.
'God!' Milt said, still looking out of the window. 'Don't you go apologising - I feel bad enough about it already.'
'I know how you felt about your scooter....' she said, but Milt turned around and interrupted her. 'I thought I did as well - but I've been thinking - now ain't that a turn-up - me thinking....' he laughed nervously and turned back to the window.
'I was a bastard Sharon - a right bastard!' There was no eye contact with her but what he was saying was heartfelt. It was enough that he was saying it. 'You know I've done some pretty bum things in my life - stuffed myself full of all kinds of junk - but the other day...well...you know I even surprised myself...I could have killed you. And I feel so lousy about it.'

There was a pause in the conversation.
'The baby's okay Milt.' Sharon was, in effect, consoling him. He turned around and looked her in the eye. 'I'm glad Sharon.' he said, 'really.'

Sharon started to well up and Milt turned back to the window.
'Anyhow, I heard that scooters are on the way out - some tickets are flashing around in tarted up minis.' He turned back to her smiling broadly . 'D'you fancy a hot mini, eh?'

Sharon said nothing but smiled and nodded furiously in agreement. Milt turned back to the window again. 'Besides - the GS needed a decoke anyway....'

On their way back to the bedside, Don and Andy's attention was diverted from Sharon and Milt as they made their acquaintance with two trainee nurses on the next ward. From the style of their hair and their body language it was immediately apparent that they were Mods. Neither Andy nor Don had seen the girls in town before that night and in the course of the conversation it transpired that, to complete their training, they had only recently been transferred from a hospital in Stevenage (a town they knew had a strong Mod contingent).

The girls were confident, self assured and with their southern accents, sounded like ambassadors from another planet: Don and Andy held court and convinced the girls that **they** were the people to be seen with in the town. They made a date to see them straight after their shift, which would finish in about an hour. Once again they were converted into a double act - Milt, it seemed, would be out of circulation for some considerable time.

As Andy chatted up the nurses and Milt was making things right with Sharon in the next ward, the scar tissue of recent wounds was slowly starting to heal.

***

FAREWELL ANGELINA

A pair of deftly wielded size 9 leather work boots with steel toecaps are capable of inflicting extensive damage to the fine flowing lines of a Lambretta LI 150 Rally Master Scooter. When such footwear was on the feet of ex-vertical driller number 911 their destructive capability was virtually unlimited.

Although Don had the bike repaired after Ralph Baldock had given it a good kicking, causing some serious damage, it never felt the same and neither he nor Andy could summon up the same enthusiasm for riding it. It seemed to handle differently and several checks on the bike's steering geometry failed to rectify its tendency to understeer.

It seemed that Baldock had his revenge after all. He thought the bike belonged to Andy (and in a way it did), after seeing him ride it home from Don's after the Bank Holiday. He vented his anger one night while it was parked in Church Walk.

They never did find out, who was responsible, but there were many in the town who were laughing down their sleeves.

If you step out, then you tread dangerously - the three of them knew that and loved the buzz it gave them.

After Don's bike had been desecrated Andy felt odd and ill at ease. There was a different feel about the streets and the atmosphere in the dance halls and clubs had changed. The pattern of their lives had altered - Milt had again left them to pursue their own lives, but this time his departure from the trio was not of a temporary nature. His absence was terminal. Their life now seemed to have taken on a "grown up" feel about it: serious and structured in its tone. It was not something he could easily define, but an uneasiness had settled on them. He knew Don felt the same way but neither had wanted, or dared, to speak about it.

*

Don was the first to break their joint silence on the subject. It was on a Monday night in early October. They were hanging over the railings at the Castle, watching the traffic pass by.

'They finish the by-pass next month you know.' Don said. His voice was as chill as the autumn air.

'Yeah.' Andy said absently.

'Then there won't even be any traffic left to watch in this place.'

'Yeah.' Andy repeated, 'Are we going down "The Green"?'

'After I've seen Tinny.' Don said, looking Andy squarely in the eye.

'Tinny - what for?' Andy looked puzzled.

'He's on about going on the continent to work the winter - some big Nottingham firm's landed a big contract, building hotels - they're crying out for steel erectors - he reckons all you need is a passport, a ratchet spanner and a head for heights.'

'So?' Andy said cagily.

'I'm thinking of going with him - 'you game?'

Andy said nothing. These were the words that he had lately realised would, sooner or later, have to be spoken.

'Apparently they can't build 'em fast enough over there - they're stacking 'em up like Meccano all down the coast - they're all Boom Towns.' Don carried on.

'Where?' Andy asked quietly.

'Er....Torre....Torremoul....Torremolinos....I think it's near Paris.'

*

Don joined the gang of building workers on the Spanish contract, lying smoothly and convincingly about his experience in the building trade; there was an employment contract which all the gang had to sign and with his signature thereon a part of the 60s was signed away.

***

HANG ON SLOOPY

Andy felt like a fish out of water.
He'd let the payments on his Vespa slip further behind - he hadn't the money to pay for the scooter and even less inclination to ride it. It was parked next to Don's Lambretta in the shed, the chrome on both machines was slowly starting to tarnish in the damp air of October. He had received a letter a couple of days ago from the finance company, formally informing him of their intention to repossess the bike - he read and binned the letter. Let it go - let it go.

The long hot summer had slipped quietly into autumn and the prospect of a cold winter stretched out in front of him - without Don or Milt. At seventeen, going on eighteen, he was beginning to feel old and vulnerable - jeez, he thought, where had the summer gone, how easily had they all let it slip from their grasp? The Mod scene had stormed in on a lion's roar and was petering out in a whimper.

Life at the factory was even more intolerable and to rub salt into wounds he hadn't been out of the town since Don had left for Spain. His life was presently confined to a couple of hundred acres of real estate.

The world, he felt was shrinking. Sharon was expanding. And "Mr. Tambourine Man" had just slid out of the bottom of the Top 50.

*

He didn't notice the post mark on the letter as he opened it or the brightly coloured stamp. He thought it was another acid laden epistle from the finance company, but he smiled as he read it:

Dear Andy,

Still getting soaked through on the scooter? What's that poem you were always spouting last summer 'Oh to be in Malaga now it's pissing down in England!'

It's bloody great down here - the job's not up to much, but the beer's cheap and the women, well they're just fantastic. I've spent the last three weeks with this Chinese girl who works in one of the hotels - I've never met anyone with skin so smooth - she's just incredible - her room's next to the fire escape. She sneaks me in and out - (in and out - get it?!!). She's only got a single bed - but I'm not complaining!!!!

Come on out here - I can get you on the site. No problem. We're short handed and the job's behind time. They'd take anybody on - even you!!

Sell the LI - anything over thirty five quid you can keep.

Write back,

Don

P.S. How's Milt and Sharon?

*

A positive attitude emerged in Andy after he had read Don's letter - he handed in his notice at the factory. It felt good as he left it all behind him on that last Friday night. He walked down the lane away from it, without a backward glance.

He had no idea of what he was going to do following Don's letter. He only knew he had to do something and his leaving the factory was the first step in some direction - wherever it might take him.

He thought he might try to get into journalism or something which had a bent towards words, to satisfy his rekindled curiosity for those strange and mysterious formations collectively described as English Literature.

He had decided to try and write down some recollections of this period in his life in a sort of journal. (Who knows, he thought, some day he might want to write a book about it.) He dug out his old fountain pen, unused since he'd blotted his way through his "O" Level Geography paper, and made the first entry in an old jotter he'd found in his bedroom:

So Don's in Spain - steel erecting (and the rest!) and Milt's going to be a father - so where does this leave me? Still out in the streets.

I suppose it'd be too dramatic to say that I'm at some sort of a cross roads, but I think, in a way, that I am. So I have to decide what I want to be - not an engineer! - a steel erector?

All I ever wanted to be was a Mod.

Mods - we had our own way - it was a matter of style really - I know some people've delighted in laughing at us - but I cry for them. But it doesn't really worry me what anyone thinks about me or what I look like. They know nothing about me or Don or Milt or any of us for that matter - about how we've lived out in the streets.

But that's all in the past now - it's what's looming up in the future that's getting to me. I've lived hour by hour as a Mod and I'm already starting to talk in months and years. Funny, I've hardly had time to think since I left school, but lately, I have been thinking and I've come to certain conclusions about the future and what it holds for me.

This prompts me to write one thing and one thing only.....

HELP!

OBS
NEWARK
1646

Post MODernisms

The author and publishers are grateful for permission to quote from the following works:-

"Can't Explain"	- words and music by Pete Townshend
"Substitute"	- words and music by Pete Townshend
"My Generation"	- words and music by Pete Townshend
Copyright ©	- Fabulous Music (Reprinted by permission of Pete Townshend)

*

The lyrics from "Go Now" by Larry Banks and Milton Bennett have been reproduced by kind permission of Trio Music Inc - Copyright Owner and Carlin Music Corporation - UK administrator.

*

"Tarantella" by Hilaire Belloc

Reprinted by permission of the Peters, Fraser & Dunlop Group Ltd

*

Alan Fletcher was a story consultant on The Who's film - "Quadrophenia" and also wrote the novel which tied in with that film.

*

The more observant among you will have noticed a couple of deliberate "non-sequiteurs" in the chronology of the story - the author craves forgiveness.

*

Dickie Valentine, one of England's best ballad singers of the 50s and early 60s, died tragically in a car accident in 1974.

*

George (Beau) Brummell, Dandy and arguably the archetypal Mod (in terms of style), died destitute in a French Lunatic Asylum on 30th March 1840.

("*A Man of Fashion, Gone to the Continent*")